When Grownups Drive You Crazy

EDA LeSHAN

MACMILLAN PUBLISHING COMPANY
NEW YORK

First Edition
Printed in the United States of America
10 9 8 7 6 5 4 3 2 1

The text of this book is set in 12 point Simoncini Garamond.

Library of Congress Cataloging-in-Publication Data
LeShan, Eda J. When grownups drive you crazy. Summary: Explores the conflicts and misunderstandings that occur between adults and children and offers advice to youngsters on understanding and dealing with the things adults do that distress them. 1. Children and adults—Juvenile literature. 2. Parents and child—Juvenile literature. [1. Parent and child. 2. Interpersonal relations] I. Title. HQ772.5.L55   1988   306.8'74   87-22005
ISBN 0-02-756340-5

DEDICATION

I was visiting Michael, who was eight years old. Later on I was going to a meeting with his mother and his father, where I was to give a speech about a book I'd written called *When Your Child Drives You Crazy*. Michael didn't seem to like that at all, and I could understand how he felt. That title sounded as if I didn't like children very much. He didn't realize that what I wrote about in that book was that parents feel as if their children are driving them crazy only when they *don't understand* their children.

When I explained this to Michael, he thought that was all right. But then I said, "I'm thinking about writing a book for children called *When Grownups Drive You Crazy*," and Michael thought that was a great idea. I explained that the book would be about how grownups can drive children crazy when children *don't understand* grownups.

When I left to go to the meeting, Michael said, "Don't forget to send me the first copy!" Then I knew I had to write this book. And the first copy is being sent to Michael.

CONTENTS

Where the Trouble Starts

My parents drive me crazy!" says Robin. "One minute they are talking about how I should always tell them the truth, and the next minute they start yelling at me when I do." Kevin complains, "My teacher makes me so angry. He tells me he wants to listen to my ideas, and then he interrupts me and says I don't know what I'm talking about!"

When I asked about fifty different young people if grownups they knew sometimes drove them crazy, they all said, *"Yes!"* It's a common feeling, but when we talk about people "driving us crazy," we can mean many different things.

Sometimes this kind of feeling is not too important and passes very quickly. Your mother tells you you can't leave the house on a Saturday morning until you clean your room, and you think she makes much too much fuss about everything having to be in order. You might mutter, under your breath, "That woman is driving me crazy." On the other hand, your mother, who has a full-time job all week and wishes she could rest over the weekend, is tired of having to tell you that your room is a mess, and she might sigh and say to your father, "That boy is driving me crazy." By the afternoon, you both have probably forgotten the whole episode.

The day your teacher gives you *three hours* of homework over the weekend, you might tell your best friend, "Mrs. Sanchez is driving me crazy." And in the teacher's lunchroom Mrs. Sanchez might be saying, "That sixth-grade class is doing such sloppy, careless work, they are driving me crazy!" Maybe on Monday she will be pleasantly surprised by your work, and you may feel proud of what you've done.

At such times, to say you're being "driven crazy" is just a way of expressing momentary annoyance. People can annoy each other briefly, without its being very important.

When Not Understanding Can Be Serious

There are other, more serious times when grownups and children really upset each other. Marty's mother told his pediatrician, "Marty is driving me crazy—I don't know what to do. I know he's taking money from my pocketbook and he lies about it."

The problem here is that Marty's mother *cannot understand* why he is doing what he is doing. His behavior will "drive her crazy" until someone helps her to understand that Marty is stealing because he's feeling very unhappy right now. His mother and father have recently separated, and he feels that nobody really cares what happens to him, that nobody loves him. Marty doesn't understand why he's taking the money, either. He doesn't want to take it, but he can't stop himself. Both he and his mother need help in understanding each other, and once they do, Marty's mother won't feel the same way at all.

Janet would never dare to say it out loud to a grownup, but she tells her best friend, "Mrs. Perry is driving me crazy. Even when I have the right answer, she never says I'm doing well, and when I make a mistake she embarrasses me in front of the whole class. She picks on me more than anyone else."

Janet's teacher is driving her crazy because Janet *cannot understand* Mrs. Perry's behavior. What neither of them is aware of is that Janet looks a lot like Mrs. Perry's younger sister, and when they were children, Mrs. Perry felt her parents loved this sister more than they loved her. Without any conscious thought of what she is doing, Mrs. Perry is being mean to Janet because she always wanted to be mean to that younger sister.

The kind of "crazy" that this book is all about is the feeling we all get sometimes when we don't understand another person. When children "drive grownups crazy," it is almost always because grownups don't understand children's behavior; they have forgotten how it feels to be a child. When grownups "drive children crazy," it is because children don't understand grownups' behavior and often think it means something that it doesn't really mean.

As you read this book, you will see that the kind of "craziness" I'm talking about is not just being temporarily annoyed, but being really quite upset about important feelings between grownups and children.

Having Many Feelings All at Once

There are, of course, many different grownups who have the capacity for driving you crazy. Some are very close and very important; others may only touch your lives once in a while. But the closer your relationship with an adult is, the more "crazy feelings" you will have, because all your feelings are stronger when you not only like but also love a person.

In order to write this book, I have had to separate different feelings, but the truth is that feelings are always all mixed up in real life. You can be scared and angry and confused all at the same time; you can love and hate a person at the very same moment; you can want to get more attention from someone and at the same time wish to be left alone. Feelings just are that way, and I hope you will remember that separating feelings into different chapters is a convenience, not a matter of fact.

Understanding Yourself and Others

What you discover as you grow up is that parents all behave differently, and that any grownup can be friendly and loving one day and bad-tempered and mean the next day. Grownups often can't answer all your questions, but there are times when they expect you to know more than you know. Sometimes you feel they are treating you like a baby, and other times they expect you to do things you can't possibly do.

When you were a helpless baby, you needed to believe grownups were perfect. They seemed so strong, so powerful. At first it seemed they could do just about *anything*, from tying shoelaces to feeding you something delicious or putting something on your gums to stop them from hurting so much when your first teeth were coming in. Your parents and other grownups seemed like all-powerful giants.

After a while, when you didn't feel quite so helpless, you began to have a sneaking suspicion they might not be so perfect, after all! At about two, you thought they were awful when they wouldn't let you go out in the snow without wearing a snowsuit and boots. And you really knew how mean they could be when they wouldn't let you eat cupcakes and soda for breakfast! When you tried to make them understand that you weren't a baby anymore and wanted to decide some things for yourself, you probably said, "No!" So sometimes they got pretty angry at you.

On the other hand, it was very hard for you to believe that you could feel safe with other people. You thought you wanted to be independent and free, but you were probably a little scared the first time you slept overnight at your grandparents' house, and the first week in kindergarten it didn't seem possible that Ms. O'Leary could take care of you.

It's not just other people who can "drive us crazy." Sometimes we drive ourselves crazy because our feelings are so mixed up!

One of the best things about beginning to understand how your parents and other grownups got the way they are is that you will begin to understand *yourself* as well. You will begin to see that all human beings have some of the same kinds of feelings and are alike in many ways. But each one is also a distinct individual, because what we inherit from our parents is unique and what happens to us after we are born is different. Learning more about adults will help you to appreciate and enjoy all the exciting differences in all the people you are going to meet later.

Getting to Know Grownups

There is no way that I can give you examples of every single thing that grownups do that can drive you crazy. What I can do is to try to give you enough examples so that you'll be able to develop certain attitudes that will help you meet such problems. I think I can help you understand grownups better, and when we understand people better we can begin to do some things about dealing with what really bothers us.

Although I will be talking about all the grownups in your life, most of the things that drive you crazy will have to do with your parents—for a very good reason. Even though you are certainly not as dependent on them as you were when you were a baby, you still need them a lot. Of all the grownups you know, you love them most, and you want them to love you most of all. Where there are strong feelings of love, there can be other kinds of strong feelings as well, feelings that can get people in trouble with each other. Later on I will talk about other people in your life, such as teachers and grandparents and doctors, but how you learn to deal with them will depend a lot on how you learn to deal with your parents.

I hope this is a book you and your parents will read together. Sharing your ideas and feelings can help you have a better relationship with each other. As I begin to talk about your parents, let me say that the love between parents and children is just about the best thing there is in the whole world, and in most ways your parents (as well as the other grownups in your life) prove their love to you every day by all the things they do for and with you. But this is a book about when they drive you crazy, so we are going to take it for granted that good and wonderful things happen a lot of the time. That's not the subject under consideration right now!

Discovering Each Parent Is a Different Person

Problems with parents began the day you were born! At first there was absolutely *nothing* you could do for yourself—you were completely helpless. And what you discovered pretty quickly was that there were big people who fed you when you were hungry and sometimes rocked you to sleep when you had a stomachache and made you feel dry and cozy when you'd been wet and cold. You couldn't even sit up alone, so they held you up with their arms while you sat on their laps. You certainly couldn't walk, but they took you out in a carriage, so you could take a look at this very interesting world.

Your first (and very accurate) impression of parents was that you needed them desperately to take care of you. There was no way you could take care of yourself, and your parents seemed like powerful giants who knew everything and controlled your life completely.

But as you grew, you could begin to accept the idea that parents and other people were human beings who were actually far from perfect. Dad could lose his temper, and Mom didn't know the answers to many of your questions, and sometimes they yelled at you and at each other.

Now you are old enough to have faced the fact that each human being can sometimes be wonderful and at other times be awful; be kind and mean, selfish and generous, loving and angry. Once you begin to realize *you* have such feelings, it isn't quite so hard to accept the fact that parents do, too. But it's not always easy, and there are times when parents can drive you crazy with the things they say and do. When that happens, trying to understand each other can help a lot. It can lead to being able to talk to each other about feelings, and that helps most of all.

Parents Are Individuals

One of the first things you began to observe about parents as you grew was that each one had different ways of acting and thinking and feeling. You probably wondered, How could that be? Weren't some things absolutely right and some things absolutely wrong? If they were old enough to become parents, why didn't they agree about how to raise children? If they were grown up, why didn't they act the same way, all the time?

What you have been learning is that parents are individual people who grew up in different homes, had different experiences, and will always have different personalities.

For example, let's say that your mother doesn't believe in spanking and your father does. You wonder why they are so different; you also know your father really loves you, so how could he hit you? What you might find out if you asked some questions is that nobody ever hit your mother when she was a child, but Dad's parents believed in spanking as a punishment. That tells you, for one thing, that when you are punished it often has less to do with what you are being punished for than with the early experiences of your parents. Once you understand that, maybe you can become brave enough to tell your father how really bad you feel when he hits you and to ask him if he could punish you in some other ways.

Understanding where your father's attitude and behavior began also can help you to feel less guilty about what you may have done and a little less angry at your father. You might even feel sorry that he went through the same thing when he was a child.

Helping a Parent Remember

Most of what parents think and do with their own children started when they were children, and if you can begin to understand that, you will find you are less confused and feel less guilty. After a bad time like being spanked by your father, perhaps you could ask him, "Did Grandpa spank you when you did something he didn't want you to do?" It might start your father remembering how it made him feel.

You can influence what happens between you and your parents sometimes by asking them questions. It will help them to remember how they felt when they were children. It also will help you to understand how they became the people they are.

Let's say your mother heaps a lot of food on your plate. You aren't very hungry, and you hate fish and brussels sprouts. She won't let you leave the table until you have finished every single thing on your plate. *It drives you crazy!*

There are a number of possibilities in such a situation. You could refuse and get into a big fight and maybe get punished far more severely than seems fair. This makes you very angry, and for the moment you really hate your mother. Feeling that way makes you feel frightened and

9

guilty, because of course you also love her a lot. When she gets very upset, you feel like an awful person who has been bad.

But there is another possibility. You could ask your mother if she had to finish everything on her plate when she was a child. You could ask her why her parents made her eat everything on her plate. Was it because her parents had been poor and food was very precious? Was it because they had come from a foreign country where they never had enough to eat? Did they tell her she had to eat all her food because there were children in some other parts of the world who were starving?

Maybe after your mother has a chance to think about it and remember her own childhood, she will be willing to make a compromise with you—that you eat half of what is on your plate, or maybe even that you only have to eat fish once in a while and no brussels sprouts at all! Helping her remember how it was when she was a child may help her understand how you feel now.

When I was a little girl, I had to finish everything on my plate. I had to eat my vegetables first, then I got my meat, and then I got my dessert. In those days people worried about having thin children—they thought it was healthy for a child to be roly-poly. One reason for this was that children used to get a lot of diseases that they no longer get, like diphtheria and smallpox, and if they did become sick, there were no antibiotics to make them well. It was very dangerous to be sick and you could stay sick for a long time, so parents wanted children to have a little extra fat to see them through the illness. Also, when I was a child my mother used to tell me I had to eat my food because of the starving children in Afghanistan. I wasn't sure what that meant, but I didn't dare ask any questions.

10

Years later, I tried to make my daughter finish everything on her plate; I made her eat food she didn't like when she wasn't hungry. I said she had to eat because of the starving children in Korea. But things have changed for the better in many ways since I was a child. First of all, my husband has no hangups about food—his mother hadn't worried as much as mine—so *he* took the plate away when Wendy was full. And then one day she asked me, "How can it help the Korean children if I eat this?" I finally came to my senses and realized I was doing something dumb just because it had happened to me when I was a child.

Helping your parents *remember* is just about the best way to change the things that drive you crazy. And when they remember, a lot of things that drive you crazy may stop happening, or at least you will understand them better and will be able to deal with them in a more comfortable way.

People Are Different

That doesn't mean that you can solve all the difficulties between you and your parents. The more close and important a relationship is, the more we are likely to be our real selves—not polite robots. Some differences between us and our parents are inevitable. We can never agree about everything.

Joyce says, "My father makes a big fuss about my table manners, but he doesn't care if my room is a mess. My mother screams about keeping my room neater, but she even lets me eat in front of the TV set when my dad isn't home. I go crazy trying to figure out what's okay and what isn't." Victor says, "My mother won't let us take any food or drinks into the living room, and my father thinks it's all right. But if I touch his tools in the garage, he has a fit. They don't get mad at the same things at all. It drives me crazy."

Wah Chin reports, "My mother thinks I should go outside and play after school, and she and my father have big screaming fights because he wants me to do my homework as soon as I get home." Jeff adds, "If I do something wrong, I'd sure rather have my father decide on the punishment than my mother! She's much more strict." Alma says, "My father swears all the time, but if I say a word my mother doesn't like, she threatens to wash my mouth out with soap. I can't figure them out."

How would you answer all these children? I hope you would say that the reason each parent is so different is that each grew up in a different home with different parents and learned different attitudes. Our parents are the first people who teach us a very important lesson about life: that people are different and that it can be an exciting adventure to try to discover what makes each person tick and how to get along with them.

We can try to clean up our rooms most of the time, but we can also recognize that we aren't such terrible slobs or bad people if we don't, and we can probably try a little harder to be kind to someone who just doesn't understand that a room filled with things we like may not seem at all messy to us. (There was a cartoon a few years ago of a little boy standing at the door of his bedroom, where everything was in perfect order, and he is shouting, *"Who messed up my room?"*) You need to remember that if your mother is always after you to clean your room, she probably had to be very neat when she was a child.

In the same way, you need to understand that almost all children get fidgety during meals and rest their elbows on the table. But to be kind to Dad, you'll try as much as possible not to kick the table legs and not to get too angry about the elbows-on-the-table business because it's more than likely his dad yelled about the same thing.

Becoming a Kind Person

It's much easier to be kind to and considerate of another person when we begin to understand some of the reasons for his or her behavior. And that is just as important a goal as any other if we want to become civilized and caring people.

Manuel said, "I wanted to yell at my father to stop pestering me all the time about whether or not I did my homework. Then, one day, when I was about ten years old, I was listening to my grandfather talk to my father. For the first time, I noticed that my grandfather was acting like a lawyer cross-examining a witness. He wanted to know exactly how my father was getting along in his job, and he kept telling him he could really do better and should have gotten a promotion. I guess I was old enough to see that my father was probably nagged a lot when he was going to school. Next time my father asked me if my homework was done, I said, 'Yes, Dad, I'm doing okay.' I didn't even feel angry. I felt sorry for how his father treated him, and I decided to ask him more questions and show him I think he's a terrific person."

Kim got into a really bad argument with her mother about whether or not she could wear blue jeans to school. Kim said it was allowed, and her mother said, "I don't care if it's allowed or not, I won't have you going to school looking like a bum!" That made Kim furious. She screamed at her mother, "You don't understand anything!

You grew up in the Dark Ages, and you're too fat to wear blue jeans, anyway!"

Kim's mother burst into tears. Being overweight was just about her most painful problem, and Kim had hurt her badly. Kim said, "Oh, Mommy, I didn't mean to say something so mean! I think you are beautiful and I love you so much!" Kim and her mother hugged each other and her mother said, "And of course I don't think you ever look like a bum! We say such awful things to each other when we're angry!" For the first week of school Kim wore a skirt and sweater. When she brought her friends home after school, though, Mrs. Berger saw that what Kim told her was true; all the other girls were wearing blue jeans. "You wear your blue jeans and I'll join a health club!" she said.

Such happy endings don't always occur; in most families it's a lot harder than that to deal with hurt feelings. But as you go on reading, I hope you will remember that learning to understand each other better is the way both parents and their children become kinder, nicer people.

When Parents Seem Unfair

One of the first times you may have noticed how different your parents are might have been when it seemed to you they were not being fair—but about different things. Sonya's mother felt that eight was too young to go to the park alone with her friends; her father thought it was all right. Vincent's father refused to let Vincent spend the money he'd been saving from his allowance on a very fancy skateboard; his mother said, "Leonard, it's really his money—if he wants to use it all up on one thing, that's his choice."

Over and over again, most children are surprised at how each parent will seem to be fair about one thing and unfair about something else. Frank told me, "I guess you might say it evens out, except when *both* parents are being unfair!"

Sometimes children feel that parents are being unfair, when they are really trying to guide and protect their children. It is natural to feel something is unfair just because it's not what you want. Philip thinks it's very unfair that he isn't being allowed to play football; his parents think they are saving him from the possibility of getting hurt. Melanie thinks her parents are being unfair when they refuse to let her go on a week's vacation trip

15

with her best friend and her parents; what she doesn't know is that her parents have heard that Mr. and Mrs. Harper are fighting quite a lot and this "vacation" might be a disaster. They don't want Melanie to be caught in a bad situation, but they can't tell her because no one knows for sure what is happening in the other family.

Fairness is often not easy to figure out. What we think about it depends on so many different experiences and attitudes that it's just about impossible to decide what is fair and unfair. But one thing is certain; children have very strong opinions about how they *feel*. And there is probably nothing that drives children crazier than to feel that their parents treat them differently from their brothers and sisters.

Brothers and Sisters

It's possible that your first awareness of parents' being unfair had to do with a brother or a sister. Maybe you're older, but your parents make you go to bed before your little brother. Or maybe your mother gives your sister a bigger piece of cake. Or maybe your father says, "Your sister pays attention in school—why are you such a daydreamer?" You may think that your parents pay more attention to a brother or a sister, or you may even feel they don't love you as much as they do another child in the family. Feeling that you are being treated unfairly can drive you crazy.

The truth of the matter is that fairness just doesn't apply among brothers and sisters. Sandra at eight may have to go to bed earlier than two-year-old Matthew because she has a hard time waking up in the morning to go to school and Matthew has an afternoon nap. Mother may give Niki a bigger piece of cake because Chrissy was told by her pediatrician that she needed to be careful about gaining weight.

You are right that parents pay different amounts of attention to different children and love them each in a different way. That should comfort you instead of driving you crazy, because it means they see each child as an individual with different needs. That kind of "unfairness" means that you and your brothers and sisters aren't all being lumped together, with your parents self-consciously trying to behave in the same way with each of you. Each person is different, and it's not unfair to treat each one differently.

Favoritism

Of course, there are some kinds of unfairness with brothers and sisters that are very upsetting. Sometimes you just know that your mother or father prefers one child, or has a lot of trouble showing love to another child. That can make you feel sad and lonely and angry. When something as serious as this is going on, you may find it helpful to think about your parents' past.

Laurie said, "One day when I was really unhappy, I told my grandmother that Mom loved my sister, Peggy, more than she loved me. I was really shocked when Grandma laughed. But then she said, 'Laurie, darling, she loves you both, but I'll tell you what's going on. You look almost *exactly* like Aunt Fay, and when she and your mother were growing up, Aunt Fay sometimes made your mother's life miserable by bossing her around. I tried to help, but I think, deep down, your mother still remembers being bullied by Aunt Fay, and because you look so much like her older sister, your mother may have a harder time showing you the affection she feels for you.' I still feel upset sometimes, but what Grandma told me helps a lot."

Max said, "I'm sure that my father prefers my older brother, Seth. He's so proud of everything Seth does—he boasts about him all the time and even talks about how handsome Seth is." I knew a family like that where there were two sons. One was tall and handsome and very athletic, and the other looked exactly like his father—short, with a big nose—and was also clumsy. The father was a very bright man who had become a doctor, but all his life he had felt ugly and awkward at sports. When he found he had a handsome, athletic son, he went wild with excitement; this son was everything he wished he could have been. When I told him that his other son felt unloved, this father looked shocked and upset. He said, "That's terrible! How could I be so stupid? While I admit I'm enjoying Brian's talents, the truth is I think I probably love Tom in a deeper way just because he's so much more like me, and I understand his feelings of inferiority because that's how I felt as a child. I need to let him know that he and I have lots of other important qualities."

Whenever you are really uncomfortable about parents' being unfair, you need to try to tell them how you feel. If you can't bring yourself to do that, sometimes another relative can help by explaining the situation the way Laurie's grandmother explained it to her. Or sometimes you can watch what happens when the whole family gets together.

At Thanksgiving last year, Nicholas noticed something very interesting. His father was very affectionate with his sister, Aunt Maureen, but he and his brother, Uncle Marvin, argued about everything and were constantly trying to prove that one was better than the other. It seems pretty clear that when Dad was growing up, he got along better with a younger sister than with an older brother. That's probably why he calls Nicholas's sister his "little princess" and is often so critical of Nicholas, whether it's about how he hits a baseball or his grades in school.

Younger, Older, or in the Middle

If you are the oldest child, you are probably often asked to take care of younger brothers and sisters. Being somewhere in the middle sometimes makes you feel that nobody pays much attention to you. And if you are younger than your brothers or sisters, your parents often expect you to wear their hand-me-down clothes. Your sister gets new school clothes every year, and you almost never have anything new to wear. Or your brother or sister is so much older that by the time you fit into his or her clothes, they are no longer the style of the clothes your friends wear. That can seem very important during a time when you want so much to be exactly like your friends.

If this happens to you, it might be a good idea to try to make a deal with your parents. It is true that children's clothes are now very expensive, and few families can afford to throw away clothes that are still in good condition. Maybe you can say you will wear the old clothes after school; maybe you can suggest that some of them might be sold at a garage sale or to a thrift shop, and whatever money is gotten can go toward new clothes. Maybe you can agree to wear hand-me-downs if you can have one new school outfit and one new pair of jeans or a party dress each fall. Maybe you can earn some money baby-sitting a younger brother or sister, or delivering newspapers, or helping paint the porch, and that money can be used for a special outfit. Parents are more likely to be thoughtful of your feelings if they see that you are also concerned about how much clothes cost.

Comparisons

One thing that drives most brothers and sisters crazy is to have parents compare them to each other. Your older brother was a terrific basketball player, and they can't understand why you are not as good. You like to do quiet things, alone after school, and your parents nag you to go out and make friends the way your older sister does. Most of all, they compare how you do in school.

If you watch closely, you may discover something very interesting. While your parents are comparing you to a brother or a sister in some area where you are not as successful, they also may be telling that brother or sister that he or she should be as good as you are at the things you do well. You may be shocked to hear a parent say to your social-butterfly older sister, "It would be nice if once in a while you stayed home and read a book the way your brother does." Parents tend to do this sort of thing without thinking about it. They want all their children to be wonderful at everything! You need to remind them this is impossible.

Lester told his father, "Dad, you better get used to it. I'm never going to want to play football just because Steve does. I'm a different person. I like swimming and tennis." Maria told her mother, "Maybe I'll like cooking when I'm as old as Eric, but I doubt it. I get too restless in a kitchen—I'm a more active type of person."

When you can accept the idea that you are who you are

20

and you're not like anybody else, your parents will begin to notice your attitude. Jeremy told his father, "You should be glad Bruce and I aren't alike. Wouldn't that be very boring?" It made his father smile. It didn't mean his father would never make comparisons again, but maybe he wouldn't make them so often.

Only Children

Children who have no brothers or sisters often feel parents are unfair in other ways. Lisa feels her parents expect her to be more grown up than she really is. There are no other children around being "childish" with her, and so her parents seem to expect her to act older than she is. She also feels it's very unfair that they always tell her when she does something wrong but hardly ever praise her for the things she does right.

Only children can help their parents remember how children behave by inviting friends to come visit overnight or to go along on a camping trip. Seeing you with others your own age helps to remind your parents you are a child. And the reason so many parents seem to pay more attention to your failures than your successes is that parents worry a great deal about a child's future. They don't worry at all about the good things, but whenever something goes wrong, they are afraid it will never get better, and they are sure it's their fault.

Threats Parents Don't Really Mean

Another kind of unfairness that drives children crazy is when a parent threatens a very severe punishment and then doesn't carry it out. Carl said, "My mother scared me to death. Just because I left my bicycle in the driveway, she said I couldn't watch any TV for three weeks and wouldn't get any allowance for a month. I got so mad at her and so upset. A few hours later she seemed to have forgotten all about it. Why do parents drive us crazy with threats they don't carry out?"

Why does nine-year-old Nancy tell her best friend she'll never speak to her again in the afternoon and call her on the phone three hours later, friendly as can be? Why does twelve-year-old Adam scream at his sister for feeding his fish when she was not supposed to—why does he yell, "I'll kill you if you ever do that again!"? Both adults and children do these things because we all get angry and lose our tempers, and then, a little later, we calm down and realize we don't mean these threats. Instead of going crazy, it's a good idea to let things cool off for a while.

When Parents Deny Your Feelings

It seems unfair to children when parents tell them to do something they just know they can't possibly do. Such as, "You must always love your little brother and be kind to him." Or, "You could do a lot better, you're just not trying hard enough." Sometimes you can assume that such statements are no more believed by your parents than by you—it's just something their parents said to them when they were children, and it is very hard to give up old habits. Sometimes, though, you have to let parents know how you feel.

Carlos told his mother, "I try to love my brother, but he follows me around like a shadow, so I can never be alone with my friends, and he broke my model plane. I just can't love him every minute."

When Connie's mother told her she wasn't really trying to learn her piano lesson assignment, Connie began to cry. She said, "I feel so tired when I get home from school and all the notes seem to run together. I'm just not a musical person." She and her mother talked it over and decided together that instead of piano lessons, Connie could try an art class that met on Saturday mornings when she wouldn't be tired after a day at school.

Sometimes parents can't tell that you are really trying hard to do something unless you tell them. Sometimes they forget that you are young and that people have different abilities. You might ask them what they did well and what they did poorly when they were children.

Random Targets

One day Dad comes home from work and he's really fuming. He tells your mother his boss was completely unreasonable and yelled at him in front of several co-workers, and he had to keep his mouth shut because he wants to keep his job. Then your father snaps at you about table manners and shouts that he wants peace and quiet so he can read his paper, and when he finds out you haven't completed your homework and are watching your favorite television show, he yells at you and turns the TV off. You figure all this is going on because he couldn't talk back to his boss, but why is he picking on you? It drives you crazy.

The truth is we all do this; we find a *random target*, someone it is safe to yell at when we are upset with someone else. Josh's mother told me that one day when he came home from school, Josh yelled at her about everything. He didn't like anything they were having at supper, and he yelled at her when she asked him to put his school clothes away, and he yelled some more when she asked him about school. She thought his teacher might have said or done something to upset him. But when he shouted, "It's none of your business!" his mother got really angry and told him he'd better cut it out or he could just go stay in his room.

Then Josh said, "If I can't yell here, where *can* I yell?" His mother laughed. "I have to admit you have a point, Josh," she said. "Sometimes I am in a terrible mood with you and Daddy when I've had a fight with the cleaners or when my secretary forgot to get some work done. I guess home is the only place we *can* let off steam and know people will go on loving us, anyway."

Confusing Messages

It can be confusing and upsetting when parents tell you not to do certain things because they are bad for you, but then they do those very things themselves. They smoke cigarettes but tell you you mustn't smoke. They don't allow you to watch television for more than an hour a night or to watch violent programs, and then they watch all evening when you go to bed. They make you promise never to take any drugs, but you know your mother is taking all kinds of medicines without the supervision of a doctor. Your father lectures you about drinking, but sometimes he comes home late from work, acting funny and smelling of alcohol. They say one thing and do something else. It drives you crazy.

24

If you can, you need to let your parents know how you feel. They will probably tell you that they limit your television because it's important for you to have time for outdoor play, reading, and homework, and that children are more likely than adults to be frightened and upset by violence. They may tell you that they have tried to quit smoking and just can't—and that's why they don't want you to ever get started.

Since you will probably be learning a good deal at school about the dangers of smoking, maybe you can bring home some of the pamphlets and other reports and ask your parents to reconsider trying to stop. You can tell them that their smoking frightens you, and it isn't good for *your* lungs when they smoke.

When parents tell you that you must not do some of the things they do because they are bad for you, they are really letting you know that while they may have problems, they don't want you to have these problems. That is a sign of love.

Sometimes Parents Get Confused about How Old You Are

There is a special kind of unfairness that is as hard on your parents as it is on you. Carmen says, "One minute my mother treats me like a baby and says I can't go out with my friends after supper, even in the summertime, and the next minute she wants me to baby-sit my twin brothers all day long. If I'm such a baby I can't stay with my friends, how can I be old enough to work?"

There are reasons why parents may treat you like a baby one minute and then expect you to behave almost like an adult the next. One is that growing up doesn't happen in a steady stream—it has its ups and downs. From your parents' point of view, there are times when you still seem to be very young and to want to be taken care of (such as when you feel really sick) and other times when they are surprised by your maturity.

Grant's father told me, "I never know what to expect. At ten years old he can have a temper tantrum like a two-year-old, and he can also be president of his fifth-grade class!" Children grow up, not in regular steps of progress but by moving backward and forward under different circumstances.

Also, when people live together every day, it's harder to notice changes that take place. Let's say you have a cousin who moves away to another part of the country, and you don't see her for two years. When she comes to visit, you are astounded by how tall and how different she is. If you had seen her every day during those two years, though, you probably wouldn't have noticed how she was growing. Your parents have the same problem. Because they see you every day they sometimes don't notice how you are changing.

When I talk to parents, they tell me how confusing it is. One mother told me, "I can't believe a child can change so much in two years—Ginny was my adorable little girl for such a short time! Now, at eleven, she has her opinions about almost everything and hardly ever agrees with me!" On the other hand, a widowed father said, "Since my wife died, I guess I have expected too much of my children. When I asked Jan to go shopping at the supermarket yesterday after school and do two loads of laundry, she burst out crying and said, 'Daddy, I'm only eleven years old! I need to see my friends—I can't be a housewife!' I realize she's got a point. She has a right to her childhood. I have to get more outside help. My children have been wonderful since their mother died, but I mustn't expect them to replace her."

Children themselves often get confused about how old they are. Bruce said, "Sometimes it seems very strange that I understand so much about computers, but I still get a funny feeling if I come home from school and there's nobody there."

It is normal to grow up in some ways and to still feel very young in other ways. Realizing this may help you to understand when your parents seem very confused about just exactly how old you are. But like Jan, you can help by reminding your parents how you feel. You can tell them when some responsibility just seems to be more than you can handle, and you can also let them know, by your attitudes and behavior, when it is time for them to recognize that you have grown and changed.

Mrs. Lucas told me, "Jed kept insisting that he could ride his bicycle to school. I was nervous about it because there is quite a bit of traffic at that time of day. I told him I would let him ride his bike to school when he showed me that he was grown up enough to be very careful and observant and wouldn't take any chances. When he asked how he could prove this to me, I couldn't think of a way to test him. He suggested we go to an arcade where there was a game that tested your car-driving skills, like the ones they have in high schools. He got a perfect score, so now he rides his bike to school!"

When you want to be treated as more mature, you need to find ways to convince your parents of how much you have grown, even if it only means getting your homework done on time and taking out the garbage without being asked and not having to be reminded to feed the dog. But there will always be some problem about being seen as a growing person by your parents. They knew you when you were a helpless baby, and they never quite get over that, even when you become an adult.

Allowances

I have almost never met a child who didn't think he or she should get a bigger allowance and have more freedom to use it without any strings attached! Liz said, "What's the good of my parents giving me an allowance if they don't allow me to spend it without their approval? It's not fair."

This seems to me to be a reasonable question. As in so many things, we often learn the most from our mistakes, and if we're never allowed to make mistakes with money, we'll never learn how to handle it. I suppose the most extreme silliness about an allowance was the mother who proudly told me she gave her children twenty-five cents a week, and they saved all their money to buy her a present on Mother's Day! It's nice to care about other people, but that was not a very sensible way to learn about using money.

This is a good subject for negotiating with parents. You might ask for a family council to discuss allowances. If you show a genuine concern for your family's finances, chances are your parents will try to be fair. You can discuss how many of your expenses (like eating in the school cafeteria or, if you live in a big city, your bus or subway fare) should be covered by an allowance and how to manage a little bit more for you to use in your own way. You need to make it clear that you understand your allowance must be based on what your parents feel they can afford. If they are having a tough time paying the rent and buying food and clothes, then of course you will have to ask for a very small allowance.

As you get older, you can tell your parents that you are willing to earn part of your allowance by doing jobs they might otherwise have to pay someone else to do, such as mowing the lawn and baby-sitting. Of course, there are certain chores that children do as part of being a family and for which they ought not to be paid. People in a family do many things for each other, just to be caring and helpful. But if both your parents (or your one parent, if you live in a single-parent family) are working hard at their jobs, there may be many special chores you could do for them to earn extra money.

In discussing a fair allowance, you might ask your parents to tell you the very worst mistakes they ever made with an allowance! My guess is that most grownups remember the times they sent in cereal box tops or ordered something from a TV advertisement, and received what turned out to be "junk." You might suggest to your parents that they probably learned a lot from that experience themselves!

THREE

When Parents Embarrass You

When our daughter was twelve years old, she decided not to go to a school dance because my husband and I were supposed to be chaperones and she was too ashamed of the way we dressed. We agreed to hide behind a pillar in the school gym!

During grade school and high school, the most important thing in the world is to be like your friends, and anything that you think will make them critical is almost unbearable. What our daughter did not understand when she was feeling so ashamed of us was that every other child in her class was just as afraid of being different and just as worried as she was about being accepted, being popular.

One way to solve this problem is to tell your friends that you know your parents are either too square or too eccentric, but there is nothing you can do about it. You are not really being disloyal to your parents. The time may come when you may actually like the way your parents look and act, but there is a period in growing up when you just can't help feeling embarrassed by them.

These kinds of feelings go away when you become more sure of who *you* are. The more you become a unique, special person, the more you will be strong enough to select friends who like the things you like—and that will most likely include your parents!

The Many Ways Parents Make You Feel Embarrassed

Because young people feel insecure and worry so much about being popular, they become very concerned with style, with looking exactly the way the "most popular" children look. It's very embarrassing to go shopping for clothes and have a parent pick out all the wrong styles for you to wear. You *know* your friends will think you look awful.

Before you let this drive you crazy, ask your mother and father to *really look* at what your friends are wearing. Remind them of how they felt about looking different when they were your age. You might get to hear some pretty funny stories—and they might even buy you more suitable clothes!

One of the most embarrassing things—and it probably happens to you quite often—is to have your parents tell you to kiss and hug some relative you hardly know, and you could just about die when they tell you to sit on Grandma's lap. Probably the best thing you can do is to say you understand that they want to show what a loving person you are, and then to suggest some ways in which you could be polite and friendly and still feel comfortable. "I'm just too old to sit on anyone's lap," you might say. "But I'll show Grandma my shell collection and hold her arm walking down the steps to the playroom."

George told his father, "Aunt Mary is so old she

smells funny, and she has hair growing on her face. She gives me the creeps, and, anyway, I hardly know her, so kissing is *out*. But I'll bake a cake for her birthday, and I'll tell her I saw pictures of her in a family album and she was a beautiful bride, which is true."

Talking about You to Other People

It can make you crazy when parents talk about you to other people even though you're standing right there. They might be boasting about your grades, or, worse yet, they might be telling about the time you fell out of the boat when you went fishing with a friend. Instead of letting you talk for yourself, they act as if you are invisible.

Sometimes this may happen because your parents are being thoughtless and insensitive to your feelings. They may be trying to make an impression on the person they're talking to, and feeling more ill at ease than you are! Or they may be hoping against hope that you won't say something that will embarrass *them*. One way of helping them to feel more at ease may be to assure them when you are alone that you *can* speak for yourself. Or you could tell them that being talked about makes you shy and uncomfortable, so would they please only talk about you when you are not around.

Parents and Your Friends

If parents treat you like a baby or scold you in front of your friends, you probably feel terrible. I don't think parents really mean to embarrass you like this—they just aren't thinking at the moment. If you simply say, "I know you need to talk about that," or "I'm really sorry I did that—could we talk about it after Maryanne goes home?" most parents will recognize this as a reasonable request and will wait. If a parent is *really* upset and won't stop the discussion, you might ask your friend to leave. Any good friend will know exactly how you feel.

It's also embarrassing when parents won't let you do some of the things your friends are allowed to do. Donald's classmates in fifth grade sometimes go to a skating rink on Saturdays; their parents leave them there and pick them up a few hours later. But Donald's parents don't allow him to go because there are older teen-agers at the rink who sometimes get too wild. Donald could not bear being made to be different from his friends. He kept begging and begging and told his parents there was nothing to worry about—nothing bad happened there. Finally his parents gave in. Mrs. Kumara said, "It makes me nervous, but I know Don is very mature and sensible for a ten-year-old."

When parents won't change their minds, no matter what you say, you will just have to wait a little longer, trying in every way possible to show them you are a responsible person. And in the meantime, you can make your friends feel sorry for you for having such old-fashioned parents who are "still living in the Dark Ages."

Sometimes, though, you may have a sneaky feeling your parents may be right, even when you complain. Phyllis said, "My parents wouldn't let me go to a party where there wouldn't be any grownups. I screamed and yelled and told all my friends how mean my parents were. But later I was sort of glad, because I found out that some of the kids were drinking punch with liquor in it, and the party got pretty rough and scary."

It may be embarrassing when parents play the heavies, but at least you can say it's their fault, not yours.

Being Asked to Perform for Company

It can really drive you crazy when parents want you to perform for guests—to play the piano or dance or recite a poem—and you feel very shy and uncomfortable. You are sure you will make lots of mistakes because you are nervous, but even more important than that, you don't like to have to "show off" to please your parents and make an impression on visitors. Why can't they just let you be yourself? Won't they love you without your having to perform? That's a good question.

One day at a pool I saw a terrified little boy being pushed into the water at the deep end. I got very angry and told the swimming teacher and the mother that I thought that was an awful thing to do. Then they got angry at me. The instructor said, "Charlie knows how to swim in deep water, and his grandmother has come all the way from California to New Jersey to see him swim." Sure enough, there was Grandma sitting near the pool. I said, "I guess you're telling Charlie that his grandmother will only love him if he swims." Charlie's mother looked shocked; she just hadn't thought of it that way. She thought Charlie would be proud to show Grandma what he could do.

Charlie's mother was partly right; some children love to show what they are learning to do, just because it feels like fun and because they are proud of their accomplishments. But other children—especially those who are shy and not too sure of themselves—are often quite miserable.

Sometimes you will find you can offer some alternative, something you'll be more comfortable doing that will still show your mother and father that you understand they are proud of you and want others to appreciate you. When I was young my mother once suggested that I play a piece on the piano for Aunt Carrie. I was *terrible* at the piano, but I loved writing plays and acting. So my brother and I made up a play instead. Perhaps you, too, can choose something you love to do instead of something that makes you nervous and shy.

One of the most important things you need to learn so that fewer things will drive you crazy is to *say how you feel*. Susan's mother told her there was going to be a big family party at her house for Grandpa's sixtieth birthday, and she wanted Susan to wear a new dress and talk to all the guests. Susan said, "I just can't—I'm too shy." At first Susan's mother got very angry and impatient. She said, "You're just being silly—there's no reason for you to be shy at your age." When Susan's eyes filled with tears, her mother became very thoughtful. Finally, she said, "Well, I'll tell you what we can do. I'll give you some jobs, so you'll be too busy to think about being shy." When Susan was concentrating on serving drinks and passing peanuts and cheese puffs, she stopped feeling shy.

There is no disgrace in feeling shy and saying so. It is a very natural way to feel when you are young. In fact, there are plenty of shy grownups and they are usually very nice people.

When Parents Make You Angry

It can be confusing and uncomfortable—and even make you feel angry—when parents seem unfair or unreasonable or when they embarrass you. But usually these are passing incidents, and your feelings can change fairly quickly.

Sometimes when you are angry, though, your feelings can be much more serious and complicated. In addition to feeling angry, you may feel very hurt, even frightened, and, most of all, guilty. Usually these angry feelings happen in situations in which you are being punished.

Can My Angry Thoughts Hurt My Parents?

Once, when my daughter was very angry at me, she shouted, "I wish you'd go away and never come back!" Then she got a very frightened look in her eyes and she added, "But don't you dare go downstairs!"

When Paul was told he couldn't go on a weekend trip to the baseball museum in Cooperstown, New York, with his friend and his friend's parents because he had hit his little sister, he was furious. He felt so mad at his mother that he thought, I wish she'd go away and never come back! Then he felt frightened and guilty; he didn't really want that to happen, and he figured he must be a terrible person if he could think something so awful. When we get angry it is natural to have such thoughts, but *thinking* something can never make it happen.

It's hard for children to realize that thoughts and words can't make something bad happen; only actions can do that. But it takes a long time to get over the belief that thoughts and words have some magical power, and this is because of the way children learn to talk. I'm sure you can't remember, but I can just imagine how your parents acted when you said your first word! There was probably wild excitement, a call to your grandparents, a big hug, and a kiss. You must have thought you had done something truly remarkable, and it was the beginning of a natural feeling that words had magical powers.

When you could say "milk," you could let people know you were thirsty and hungry. When you learned to say "I love you" or "Thank you," everyone smiled and was very friendly. But when you learned to say "No, I won't" or "Go away!" all of a sudden people's faces changed and they weren't friendly at all. And if you said certain swear words you'd heard in nursery school, boy, was there a terrible reaction! It certainly seemed clear that words could make all kinds of things happen.

It is very important to learn that all kinds of angry thoughts are normal, but they cannot make anything bad happen. It is only things we or others *do* that can make things happen.

Am I a Bad Person?

Barbara said, "When my mother screams at me about something, I feel angry, but I also feel that I'm a bad person." Most children have such feelings, which can go on for a long, long time. We love and need our parents so much that we find it hard to believe they could be wrong. Any time parents tell children they are bad, the children usually take it more seriously than their parents.

When I was ten years old, I took something from a friend's house—a toy she'd gotten as a birthday present. My parents found out and scolded me, and I was sure I was a terrible person. When I grew up and studied child psychology, I found out that most children take some things that don't belong to them. While it was fair that I had to return the toy and be punished, I wish my parents could have explained that I wasn't a bad person; I was just too young to have learned how to control such an impulse when I wanted something very badly. I didn't figure that out until I was a grown woman.

When parents use physical punishment, it is logical for you to feel very angry. If you hit your younger brother, they say, "You mustn't hit someone who is smaller than you are," but if they hit you, they are hitting someone smaller than they are. Chances are that when you get spanked, or when you get the feeling that your mother or father couldn't possibly love you *and* be so mad at you, you may go to your room and lie down on the bed and cry. I remember doing that. I was angry and yet I felt whatever had happened must have been my fault.

Juan told me his father used to beat him with his belt when he was a child. Juan said, "I was so angry, I wanted to kill him. But the truth is, I never really doubted that I deserved what he did to me. It has taken me twenty years to realize I never deserved such treatment."

The important thing for you to understand is that anger in response to punishment is normal, and that even when the punishment is fair, it is normal to feel guilty as well as angry. It doesn't mean you are a bad person.

Not All Punishments "Fit the Crime"

The things that make us most angry are being punished severely for something that doesn't seem all that serious, or being punished for something we didn't do, or being punished in different ways on different days. Dennis said, "I never know what to expect. One day my father will yell at me and say I can't watch television for a week if I forget to clean out the cat box, and a month later when the same thing happens, he will just remind me in a quiet voice. It sounds crazy, but even when he's nice I get angry from not knowing what to expect!"

We have to remember that parents have moods just as children do; they have their good days and bad days, too. They are also very likely to punish you most severely for the same things they were severely punished for when they were children. That probably explains why you sometimes think they punish you too much for some minor wrongdoing and hardly make a fuss when you've done something that you feel is really wrong.

Parents are not perfect, and so punishments can often be unfair and confusing. Just remember that doing something wrong doesn't mean you are a bad child—it only means that you are too young to have learned to control yourself as you will be able to do when you are older.

When I talk to parents, I try to encourage them to say to

their children, "If you are too young to be able to stop what you are doing, I will help you stop." That "help" may be losing some privilege or staying in your room for a while to think about what you have done. But when they say "too young" instead of "bad," you don't feel so guilty.

Nothing can make us do more wrong things than the belief that we are bad. Juan, who was beaten with his father's belt, is an example of this. Feeling that he must be a very bad person, he hated himself, and the more he hated himself the more he got into trouble. He joined a gang in his neighborhood when he was seven. By the time I met him he had just come out of prison after getting into serious trouble. He and I were working hard to help him begin to like himself so that he would feel he had a right to a better life.

Being punished severely and feeling angry and guilty can make a person grow up hating him- or herself. If our parents make us feel we are bad, we begin to punish ourselves even more than they punish us. One of the hardest things for parents to remember from their own childhoods, because such memories are so painful, is that when a child does something the child knows is wrong, that child feels guilty even before being punished. The punishment sometimes even brings a certain sense of relief, because the child feels he or she deserved it.

Talking It Over

There are many parents who are able to listen to you express your feelings about how you are disciplined. They are willing to listen when you feel you have been treated unfairly; they can hear you when you say you are feeling very sorry about something you have done, and you are punishing yourself. Some parents can even begin to look back and tell you how they felt when they were punished as children.

But you would know I was lying if I said it is always possible to talk to all parents about their and your feelings. Some parents have had such bad experiences with punishment in their own childhoods that they just can't talk about it and can't allow themselves to remember. The important thing in such cases is to understand that you are not a bad person and will not grow up to be a bad person. You are young and you make mistakes, but hating yourself is never the answer. You can try to improve your behavior, but you will never be a perfect person. Your parents are proof of this!

Being endlessly lectured at by a parent can drive you crazy. Many parents don't believe in severe punishments because they know it can make a child hate him- or herself. So instead they make long, long speeches. Unfortunately, sometimes the things they say can hurt you even more than a spanking! Or the lecture goes on for such a long time you begin to think that at least a severe punishment would have been shorter and over with sooner. It can also get pretty boring.

But if you remember that your mother or your father is probably trying to treat you in a more civilized and caring and understanding way than was true in his or her childhood, you might begin to realize how much he or she must love you.

Becoming a Civilized Person

One of the reasons children so often feel they deserve punishment, whatever form it takes, is that in most cases it is true that discipline is a form of love. Few things can make you more angry than having a parent say, "This hurts me more than it hurts you." But behind that expression is usually a genuine belief on the part of a parent that he or she is doing something that will help you to grow up to be a civilized person. The methods may sometimes be less than helpful, but the goal is a loving one.

Parents have to discipline children, not because children are bad, but because part of a parent's job is to teach children how to behave so that they don't hurt themselves or others. It takes a long time to learn to behave in acceptable ways, so parents must keep giving reminders. Some reminders may be stern but fair; some may make us feel we are terrible; some can make us furious. What matters most of all is that even the most misguided parent thinks what he or she is doing is done for love. Instead of thinking of yourself as a bad person, remember you must be quite lovable if parents are so concerned about how you grow up.

Parents Who Don't Tell the Truth

When parents lie, it can drive a child crazy and cause a lot of anger. Andrew said, "I could tell from my mother's and father's faces that my grandfather was probably going to die, but they kept telling me he was going to get better." Ellen said, "I asked my mother if she and my father were going to get a divorce when I heard them fighting all the time, and she said, 'No.' The next thing I knew, my father was moving out." Barry said, "My father kept telling me how hard he worked when he was my age and what terrific grades he got. My grandfather told me my father got lots of D's and F's when he was my age!"

Most parents don't lie to be mean. Andrew's parents thought they could protect him from the pain of his grandfather's dying. They were wrong, but the wish to protect someone you love from pain is natural. Ellen's mother really hoped she and Ellen's father could save their marriage. Her "No" was a kind of wishful thinking; she was trying to protect herself as well as Ellen. And it's not too hard to understand that Barry's father thought he could make his son want to do better by making him think he had been a good student. Actually, if his father had been able to tell the truth, that might have helped Barry a whole lot more. Knowing his father didn't do such great work in grade school and yet had turned out to be a pharmacist might have comforted Barry and given him hope that he, too, would get to be a better student. But his father just didn't know that.

The best way to help parents understand that the truth is easier for you to handle is to tell them. Andrew needed to say, "I can tell from your faces that Grandpa is dying. I want to go see him and tell him how much I love him. I have a right to cry, too." Ellen might have said, "I get scared when you and Daddy fight because so many children in my class have divorced parents. But if that's going to happen, I need to know about it."

Barry told his father, "Grandpa let the cat out of the bag! He told me you had trouble in fourth grade, too. But I think I'll be able to figure out long division after a while—after all, you grew up to be a very smart person!" Barry's father was not exactly overjoyed. In a way he felt he'd been betrayed by his own father. But when he saw how relieved and happy Barry was, he didn't say anything.

Another thing that bothers children is when parents don't tell them about important things that are going to happen. Louis said, "My mother and father knew we were going to move long before they told me. When I found out my father had gotten a better job, it turned out the job was two thousand miles from where we were living and we were moving in three weeks! I was so shocked. It takes a long time to get used to such news. I was scared I wouldn't make new friends, and I felt I didn't have time to say good-bye to all the people and the places I'd known since I was a baby."

Sometimes parents will keep a secret so long that you learn the truth from someone else. Edith said, "It made me so mad. My aunt Millie spilled the beans that my mom was pregnant, and I think my mother should have told me first, before anyone else. After all, it was my life that was going to change more than Aunt Millie's!"

A more serious result of being too secretive can occur when a child finds out from a cousin or a friend that he or she was adopted. There is a natural feeling of shock and betrayal; why wouldn't a parent tell you about such an important matter? Probably for the same reason they sometimes lie; they may think they are being protective even when this is not really helpful.

Louis's parents may not have wanted him to worry for months and months about moving. Maybe they thought it would affect his schoolwork; they may have wanted to make his period of unhappiness as short as possible.

Some people are superstitious—they think if they talk about some good thing that is going to happen to them, something may go wrong. It is possible that Edith's mother felt this way. Also she may have been afraid that Edith would be embarrassed to find out her mother was pregnant twelve years after Edith was born. Some children who are almost in their teens find it kind of weird to imagine a mother getting pregnant—she seems too old for that to be happening. Maybe Edith's mother was waiting for the "right moment" because she felt a little shy about this news herself.

Sometimes parents have a right to keep secrets because they feel some things are private between themselves. Other times they keep secrets because they feel you are too young to deal with certain problems. Raymond said, "My mother tells me more than I want to hear about how she and my dad feel about each other. Some things should be private." Bonnie said, "One day my father came home all excited and happy because he got a job. I found out he'd been out of work for two months. At first I felt hurt and angry that nobody told me, and then I was glad because I would have been so frightened if I'd known." If you can remember that sometimes you may not want to hear the whole truth, it may help you at least to understand when parents don't tell you everything.

Broken Promises

There is one thing that can make young people so angry they don't even want to try to understand why their parents do it, and that's to have parents break their promises. Larry said, "I can understand if my parents have to break a promise about going to a baseball game because my father gets the flu. What I don't understand and what drives me crazy is when they promise in November that I can go to sleep-away camp next summer, and then break their promise in May."

Sometimes a plan or an idea sounds all right when it is a long way off, but as the time draws nearer, it doesn't seem so great after all. Or maybe circumstances have changed;

46

a promise may have to be broken because the car stops working and money saved for a vacation must be used for a down payment on a new car.

If Larry were to ask about the change of heart about camp, his mother might say, "I wasn't thinking clearly then, but if you go away, your sister will be all alone all summer." Such a reason might still make Larry angry, but at least now he has something he can discuss with his parents. Maybe he could go away for only two weeks or a month; maybe his sister could go to a day camp run by a nearby YMCA. Perhaps he can let his parents know how hard it is for a boy of nine to *always* have to consider the needs of a seven-year-old sister—maybe he deserves some time off for good behavior!

Sometimes parents make promises they really *wish* they could keep, such as telling you they will get you a bicycle for Christmas, and then finding there have been too many other expenses. Sometimes a parent will promise to get off from work to come see you in a school play, and then find out there is a very important meeting at work that day that can't be missed. Parents can be dreamers, too! In wanting you to be happy, they may sometimes make impossible promises. It is natural for you to feel angry and disappointed. But if you remember that they, too, wish it could have happened, the anger doesn't last very long.

Privacy

It can really drive you crazy—and make you very angry—when parents invade your privacy: when you find out your mother has read your secret diary, or your father has listened in on a conversation with a friend on an extension phone, or they've been looking through your drawers and closets for things you are not supposed to have. Sometimes the invasion of privacy occurs accidentally, such as when a parent decides that you have too much "junk" in your room and starts to clean up.

"In my diary I made up some stuff," Toni said, "about a boy in my class, and I wrote that he was kissing me and we were sort of necking a little. Most of it wasn't even true, but the next thing I know, my mother is screaming at me, don't I know I could get pregnant? I think she's gone crazy, and then I realize she must have read my diary. I was so ashamed at first and then I was furious. I felt like I'd never trust her again."

Dan said, "Jerry and I met at camp and we started writing to each other during the winter. Sometimes we wrote 'dirty jokes' to each other. It didn't really mean anything—we were both sort of showing off. But when my father told me he and the camp counselor wanted to talk to me, I realized my father must have read one of the letters. It made a big problem out of nothing, but the worst part was I couldn't believe my father could be so sneaky."

As their children approach adolescence, most parents get pretty nervous. They know you will be greatly influenced by the things your friends do and say; they know you are going to be facing more dangerous situations, and they are not at all sure they have prepared you for the problems you may have to deal with. They wonder whether, when you are a teen-ager, you would pay attention to a drug dealer outside the school building in order to act like a big shot. Would you go for a drive with someone who piles the car full of friends and goes seventy-five miles an hour? Would you drink beer and get drunk at someone's party and make so much noise that the neighbors call the police? Would you "make out" with someone because you have a friend who says you're "chicken" not to do it, even though you know you are a long way from being ready for such an experience?

When parents invade your privacy, it is probably because they *do* remember what happened to them when they were your age! They want to protect you from the painful experiences they had. They worry because they feel they will not have done a good job as parents if you get into trouble of any kind.

There are at least three ways in which you can stop parents from invading your privacy. The first way is to reassure them as much as you can that you understand the things they are worrying about and expect to be careful.

The second thing you can do is to hide private things where parents won't find them! Very often young people leave things lying around that they really don't want to share with their parents, but they also feel guilty and want to be found out. When asked, Toni admitted she did have a key for her diary but she didn't bother to use it, and Dan realized he had left Jerry's letter open on his desk. It is a normal part of growing up to have secrets with your friends, but maybe these are better shared in person than over the phone or through the mail!

Secret thoughts and feelings are nothing to be ashamed of. Part of becoming an adult is fantasizing, or imagining, how your feelings will change as you grow up. There is no reason to feel guilty about your private thoughts, so you don't need to expose your secrets in order to be punished. Sometimes we seek punishment because of feeling guilty.

Probably the most important thing you can do about having a right to some privacy is to respect the privacy of others in your family. This means not borrowing your mother's skirt without permission; not listening in on phone conversations between your father and grandmother, even if it's juicy stuff about your Aunt Natalie, who is going off to marry "a much younger man." It means *not* using a sister or brother's belongings without permission, and *not* reading anybody else's mail.

Sometimes invading a parent's privacy can be pretty upsetting. Ginny found the love letters her father wrote to her mother when he was away in the army before they were married, and reading them made her very uncomfortable. Norman discovered a letter his father had written to his family in case he got killed when he had to do a dangerous flight as a test pilot. By the time Norman read the letter, the flight was over, but the letter wasn't dated and Norman thought it was something that would happen in the future. He began to cry, which was how his mother found out about the letter. The whole family was in for a few very upsetting days.

While you try to reassure your parents that you are a sensible person who won't take dangerous chances, you might also try to help them remember how they felt when they were young and somebody read a diary or some personal letters they had written. If they say they didn't mind, ask them to think about it some more!

Parents Who Can't Accept Your Real Feelings

One of the things that probably has made you angry from the time you were very young is to have parents tell you that you are not feeling what *you* know you *are* feeling. When parents deny your real feelings, it can make you not only angry, but also lonely.

The first time your mother took you to see a dentist, she

might have said, "There is *nothing* to be afraid of," but you felt afraid, anyway. It was a lonely experience because your mother didn't seem to understand how you were feeling. The same thing could have happened when you were five years old and your father said, "You are too old to need a night light anymore." You knew you weren't that old at all—the dark shadows and strange noises still scared you at night.

When your parents were children they had many fears, too, and sometimes these were so frightening that they don't want to remember how they felt. The father who says a child is too old for a night light may just be repeating what his father said to him, but he has forgotten how it made him feel. Sometimes parents think they can make you be brave by telling you there is nothing to be afraid of, but just the opposite is true. When a parent says, "I know you feel scared," that makes you feel better! At least someone understands how you are feeling.

When my daughter was about four years old, she was afraid of the dark, even with a night light and a light on in the hall. I wasn't being very smart when I said, "There is *nothing* here to be afraid of." My daughter was smarter than I was. She said, "I'm not afraid of *your* dark—I'm afraid of *my* dark!" She taught me a very valuable lesson, one I have never forgotten. Each of us has a right to our real feelings, and it will be helpful to your parents if you remind them of this.

Feelings Can Make You Sick

Julia said that one day she was really feeling sick and didn't want to go to school. She had a stomachache and a headache. That day there was going to be a math test in school, but she felt much too sick to get up. Her mother took her temperature and said, "You are not really sick and you have to get up and go to school." Julia got out of bed, but before she could get to the bathroom she began to throw up. Then her mother was *really* angry. She said, "I know you just don't want to take that test. There's nothing really wrong with you."

Julia answered, "Remember the day you were starting a new job and you got such a terrible headache? Your head really hurt, but *you* didn't have a fever, either!" Julia's mother finished cleaning up and then sat down, thinking. "You're right," she said. "An illness is real even if it comes mostly from feelings."

Sometimes we get sick from a virus; sometimes we have a sore leg from falling. And sometimes feeling upset can make us sick. Feeling nervous or sad or excited can cause physical changes in our bodies that are very real.

Julia's mother said, "Yes, you really *do* feel sick, but do you remember that I went to work, anyway? I took an aspirin, and I told myself it was all right to be scared of a new job. I'm going to give you something to settle your stomach, and it's all right to be scared of that test. It won't be the end of the world if you don't pass it—all you can do is try." Julia breathed a deep sigh of relief. She got a C on the test, but she was sure she would have gotten a D if her mother hadn't helped her accept her fears.

Words Can Hurt

It is natural to feel angry when parents don't seem to understand all kinds of feelings that seem so real to you. If Mom or Dad tells you that you are "bad" or "lazy" or "selfish," they don't seem to understand that you are very hurt by their words and usually feel awful enough already about whatever has happened. They don't seem to understand that you get very frustrated when there is something you want to do well, but you can't because you don't yet have the skills you need. The idea in your head may be way ahead of what you can actually do.

One nine-year-old boy got furious because his mother made a big fuss over a sailboat he'd made in shop at school. When she said, "Oh, Tony, this is the most beautiful boat I've ever seen!" Tony answered grumpily, "It's no good at all. You're just saying that because you love me!" The vision he'd had in his head was something he probably wouldn't be able to accomplish for quite some time.

Sometimes parents don't seem to recognize your real feelings when they want you to share some activity with them that you don't enjoy at all, such as baseball or cooking or listening to classical music or fishing or going to the ballet. They can't seem to realize you prefer soccer or painting or reading or going to the planetarium. Sometimes if you go along with them for a while, you may find that even if their interests are not yours, you like being with them when they are feeling happy. Sometimes you may even get to like some of the things they want to share with you. Other times you need to remind them of the things *you* want to do.

When parents are unable to get in touch with your feelings, especially when you are most upset, it is a sign that they have forgotten how they felt when they were young. Mitchell came home from school one day and didn't say hello to his mother; he just dashed up to his room and slammed the door. His mother came after him and said that he was very rude and that she wanted him to set the table for supper. When he said he was too tired and just wanted to be left alone, Mitchell's mother said, "Well, if you're too tired to set the table, I guess you're too tired to eat!" Later Mitchell's sister came home from school, and she asked her mother if Mitchell was home yet. When her mother said Mitchell was behaving like a rotten kid, his sister said, "I guess you didn't hear what happened. His teacher accused Mitch of cheating on a test. The other kids told me it was another boy and Mitchell wouldn't tell on him."

It's a good idea to let people know why you are feeling bad, if you can, but sometimes you may not be sure of the reason yourself. In that case you might say, "Even I don't know what's the matter with me today—I just need to be alone for a little while." You might add, "Didn't you ever feel lousy and not know why?" An honest parent just *has* to answer "Yes"!

Listening

Julia's mother paid attention when Julia said she felt sick from being frightened, and that made all the difference to what happened. But often parents don't seem to be paying attention or listening at all. You are trying to tell them something important and their minds seem to be a million miles away. Bill's mother told me, "Bill scared me to death one day. I was talking to a friend, and he kept trying to interrupt. I paid no attention until suddenly he let out a scream at the top of his lungs. Needless to say, he got my full attention! Then he said, 'I got chosen captain of the baseball team!'"

There are usually better ways to get attention than by screaming. Maybe you can just say, "I can see you have other things on your mind right now, but when you have the time, there is something I really need to tell you." And remember that you'll have a better chance of getting a parent's attention when you really need it if you don't keep breaking into every conversation. A friend told me, "The children who live next door interrupt every conversation I try to have with their mother, and after they have shouted us down, it turns out they want us to look at a toy truck or watch them on the swing for the hundred and fiftieth time. It gets very annoying. I don't know how their mother ever knows when they have something important to say."

You may get pretty annoyed by a parent's not listening, but it's usually not something that is worth getting very angry about. The more you can be understanding of another person's feelings, the more he or she will probably be able to pay attention when it is very important to you.

Nagging

Sometimes you may wish your parents would pay *less* attention to you, especially when they start nagging you about doing something. Often these are things that they think are important but that don't seem important to you at all—such as hanging your clothes up in the closet or cleaning your room or doing your homework or drying the dishes. If you are in the middle of doing something you think is interesting and important, like finishing a game or trading baseball cards, it can drive you crazy.

While it is true that some parents can be unreasonable and frequently don't respect what you are doing, the truth of the matter probably is that *you* are driving *them* crazy because you often forget to do the chores that need to be done. The best answer to nagging is to do the job as quickly as possible so that you can get back to doing what you want to do, or to promise (and mean it!) that you'll do it the minute you are through with what you are doing.

However, there are extreme cases of nagging, where it may seem that no matter what you do, one or both parents are after you all the time about *something*. Chances are, in such extreme cases, that the nagger is feeling more dissatisfied with him- or herself than with you. A mother is more likely to nag when she feels the artwork she delivered to the head of her department at her advertising firm just didn't come out right, no matter how hard she tried; a father may be more likely to nag a lot when he's just lost a case in court; a mother may nag you constantly when what she's really upset about is a silly argument she had with her mother.

When you honestly believe that you are being criticized and nagged far more than you think makes any sense, it might be a good idea to just wait awhile until things cool down and then try to talk about it. But what is most important is to remember that what is happening is not your fault. If you have a right to your moods and are sometimes unreasonable, the same thing is true for parents, who are also human!

Wanting to Be Treated Politely

A common source of anger in young people is the fact—and it is a fact—that not all adults treat children with the same courtesy and good manners they use when they're dealing with other adults. I once saw a man I knew screaming at the top of his lungs and chasing a little boy around a store. When I asked him who the child was, he said, as if I were some kind of idiot, "Why, he's my *son*, of course! Do you think I'd yell like that at somebody else's child?"

In a number of mental health clinics where psychologists and psychiatrists and social workers try to help families with their emotional problems, an interesting experiment is sometimes carried out. The parents may be asked to keep a tape recorder going for several days, wherever they go in their home. When they listen to the tape later, they are often surprised by how different their voices sound when they talk to other adults and when they talk to their children. One father said, "It was a great shock. The tone of voice I often used with my kids I could *never* have used with anyone else. I wouldn't have a friend left and I certainly would have been fired from my job!"

Parents can make fun of you or belittle you or not consult you about things that affect you or yell at you in ways you never hear them do except with you. At the same time they expect *you* to be polite when you speak to them. It can make you feel very hurt and angry.

This is another area in which parents have forgotten their own childhood. They behave this way because when they were children their parents often did the same thing to them. Mrs. Colman told me, "I remember how angry I got when my parents were always reminding me to say 'please' and 'thank you' to them and to every other adult I met, and yet they rarely said it to me. I'm just beginning to realize I do the same thing to my kids. I'm trying to watch myself. You can't teach children to care about other people's feelings unless you care about theirs." Parents *can* learn to do things differently from the way their own parents behaved, and in some calm and friendly moment, you might let your parents know how you feel.

There are many more things that can make you feel angry, but whatever the specific incident may be, the important thing to remember is that people—both parents and children—get angry when they are tired or unhappy or impatient, or (in the case of parents) when they are behaving out of habits learned in childhood. Such behavior does not mean that people are bad—only that they are human and can't be perfect. Robots can be perfect, but people can't. And in spite of the bad times, it is far better to be a human being than a robot, because along with feelings like anger there also can be feelings of tenderness and compassion and courage and—most of all—love.

When Parents Frighten You

There are so many different kinds of fears, some that pass quickly and others that can be very important and serious. Because parents are so important to you, things they say or do can sometimes frighten you.

Margo feels frightened when she hears her parents arguing about money or where to go on a vacation or because one thinks the other isn't helping enough with housework. In her fourth-grade class there are seventeen children out of thirty whose parents are divorced, and every argument or disagreement makes her wonder if her parents might get divorced. But most of the time there seems to be so much love in her family—and so much freedom to talk about feelings—that she gets over her fear. It's the kind of fear many children have, and when it doesn't seem to have any basis in fact, it passes.

When Parents Keep Secrets

Secrets can make you feel frightened. You may have seen a parent crying and been told it had nothing to do with you, but you can't help wondering if your parent is mad at you or if maybe your parents don't love each other anymore and are going to get a divorce.

Grownups *can* have problems that have nothing to do with you, and when they won't tell you what is going on, they are usually trying to protect you. When Kerry sees her mother walking around sniffling, with red eyes, it may be that her mother and father did have some kind of argument or misunderstanding and they want to work things out privately. Unless this becomes a constant behavior, there is probably nothing to get too worried about. It is impossible for two people to live in perfect harmony all the time, even if they love each other.

Bill's dad seems to have a faraway look in his eyes at suppertime and isn't the least bit interested in the fact that Bill got an A on his history report. Bill thinks maybe he did something wrong. But what he doesn't know is that his father is having trouble at work. He's worried about his job and doesn't want to frighten his wife or Bill. Children often think that after people get married they should live "happily ever after." But all families have problems.

When parents behave in unusual and mysterious ways, it might be a good idea to say, "It would make me feel much better if you would tell me why you feel so bad. It scares me not to know." Parents sometimes forget that not knowing what is happening is much more frightening than any truth they might tell you.

When Parents Don't Act like Parents

Sometimes it can be upsetting when parents get very silly. Beverly was frightened when her parents would dance around the room, singing very loud. You want your parents to act like parents so they can help you to become a steady person. When they seem silly or childish, children wonder if their parents can really take care of them. It's a natural fear, but parents need to relax sometimes, and it doesn't mean they forget they are parents.

Another thing that probably frightens you is to have parents believe you when you lie about something, or not punish you when you know you did something wrong! As children are growing up, they know they can't control themselves and behave well all the time, and it is frightening to think that no one will help them.

Peter was visiting the house of his best friend, Sam. Peter felt that Sam was exactly the kind of boy he wished he could be. Sam was smart in school and handsome and the girls all thought he was wonderful. He was also a great athlete. It just seemed to Peter that Sam had *everything*. While Sam went to get some milk and cookies, Peter saw a paperweight on Sam's desk—the kind that looks like a snow scene when you shake it up. Suddenly Peter felt he just had to have that paperweight, and so he picked it up and stuffed it into his jacket pocket.

The next day Sam asked Peter if he had taken it. Peter's mother heard the conversation and was very angry at Sam. She said, "How could you even *think* that Peter could do such a thing to you, when he likes you so much?" But at that moment Peter was wishing his mother would say, "That was a terrible thing you did, Peter—give it back this minute!" He felt so guilty he wanted to be punished, and his mother's confidence in him only made him feel much worse!

It's actually comforting to feel that parents will help you to control actions you know are wrong when you can't stop what you are doing. Sometimes children will do worse and worse things just to force a parent to punish them because they are feeling guilty and want to get a parent's attention.

When Melissa's parents had company, the guests would put their coats and pocketbooks in her parents' bedroom. During the evening, Melissa would get an over-whelming desire to take money from the pocketbooks. She never took very much, and she felt horribly guilty, but she couldn't stop herself. One evening she heard the guests coming down the hall, but she didn't stop what she was doing and she was caught. Everyone was shocked and her parents spanked her very hard after the company left. Melissa was so relieved to be found out that she didn't even mind being spanked. She may have felt better for that moment, but what Melissa really needed was help in finding out *why* she had this strong impulse to take the money. Maybe if her parents hadn't been so surprised, they might have had a chance to think about how they could help her.

Trying to get caught for doing something you know is wrong is not a very good solution to a problem. It might be a better idea to tell your parents you feel bad about something you did and you want them to help you not to do it again. Most parents will feel that telling the truth is far more important than any mistake you might have made, and you will have given them an important mes-sage—that you need their help.

All Kinds of Fears

Many things can make you feel afraid. Nightmares can frighten you; the illness of a grandparent can frighten you; television programs can be very frightening—probably news programs can be just as or more frightening than violent stories. Finding out that a brother or a sister, with whom you have had plenty of battles, has been hurt in a car accident can just about scare you to death.

There is one very important thing you can do that helps to relieve any kind of fear; you can *take action*. Let grownups know how you feel; paint some pictures for Grandma in the hospital; bring homework and library books to the sister or brother who has casts on both legs; try to earn some money after school to help with finances when a parent is out of work. Action makes the fear more bearable. This is especially true with the things that frighten you on the news programs. You can write articles for your school paper about poisons we are burying in the ground; you can have a cake sale or plan a special show to raise money for starving children; you can give part of your allowance to organizations that are working for peaceful solutions to international problems.

When Parents Are Angry

The worst kinds of fears can be caused by the things that happen between you and your parents. For example, one day in a supermarket, I heard a mother say to her little boy, who looked about seven years old, "If you touch one more thing, I'm going to chop off your arm!" At another time, on a beach, I heard a father say, "If you don't stay out of the water when I tell you to, I'm going to kill you."

When children hear things like that, they sort of know their parents don't really mean what they're saying, but usually they aren't absolutely sure.

When parents lose their tempers and scream and yell, it can make you afraid. Sometimes they get so mad they say things that hurt your feelings. At the moment you wonder if they hate you. Except in unusual circumstances, you need to tell yourself that when people are tired, frustrated, impatient, angry, they say and do things they later regret. By now this has certainly happened to you, too.

Serious Problems

What frightens children the most is when parents are out of control. Arlene said, "When my father gets drunk and starts hitting my mother and throwing things around the house, I feel angry, but most of all I'm scared! I feel *I* must have done something terrible, and then I feel, Who is going to take care of me? Will anyone come and save me? I feel as if I have no father when he changes into this ugly person, and that I have no mother, either, because she doesn't do anything about it."

Things that happen that are very frightening usually require help from other people. One of the hardest things for any young person to face is that sometimes parents don't act like parents for serious reasons, and at such times a child may need to get help from other grownups in order to grow up safely.

When a parent drinks so much that it is clear he or she is an alcoholic, not just an occasional drinker, you feel afraid and helpless and even guilty, as Arlene said she felt. But no child is ever responsible for the upsetting things that happen to a mother or a father. No one can make someone else an alcoholic, for example. And you are not helpless; you need to talk about your problem with a teacher or school nurse or guidance counselor or a grandparent or an aunt or anyone you choose whom you love and trust a lot. He or she will be able to help you find a group of other young people—such as Al-Anon, which is part of Alcoholics Anonymous—where you can talk about your feelings with others who are having similar experiences. Once alerted to the problem, other adults also can begin to try to help your parent—to encourage him or her to get the care he or she needs to overcome this illness.

When stress is very great, the anger that you feel at something a parent is doing may turn to fear. It may make you angry if you know your mother is taking a lot of tranquilizers without seeing a doctor, but if she begins to sleep all day and can't take care of you, that is frightening. That is also a time when you need to tell a grownup, and there are now many groups to help drug addicts as well as their children. What is most frightening is that when a parent drinks too much or takes drugs, there is usually a great change in his or her personality.

Parents Who Abuse Their Children

There are some parents who had such an unhappy time growing up that they are really unable to control what they do to children. While an occasional spanking when a parent is really very angry is not the end of the world, any mother or father who beats a child or hurts a child in a serious and dangerous way is someone who is very sick in his or her feelings. If a child is being badly hurt by a parent, there is no question but that this child must get help from other people.

Fran said, "My father got so mad and shook me so hard, I fell against the wall and broke my arm. I'd heard about child abuse in sixth grade, and I knew my father didn't just have a bad temper. He slapped my mother a lot, and once he held my brother near a lighted stove and burned his hand. But I was sure that if I told anyone, they might put my father in jail or I would be sent to live someplace else, and I loved my father, in spite of everything. When he was in a good mood, he was wonderful to us."

There is much greater understanding of child abuse now than ever before. We now understand that an adult who hurts a child has a very serious emotional illness. Almost always this is a person who suffered some kind of abuse as a child and was never helped to understand what was happening and never got over it. We also know that such a person can almost always be helped by someone who is trained to deal with these kinds of problems.

There is not a single child in all the world who deserves to be abused. "Blowing the whistle" on this kind of behavior is not being disloyal or unloving to a parent; it is helping a parent face a serious problem. Seeking help is a way of saving the family, not destroying it. Now there are special groups all over the country to help families in this kind of trouble. Whenever it is humanly possible for a parent to accept treatment, every effort will be made to keep a family together.

There is another kind of child abuse that is even more frightening. This happens when a parent wants to play with your body, or have you play with his or her body, in special private places. Helen told her favorite aunt, "I'm old enough to take a shower all by myself, but sometimes Daddy makes me take a bath, and he touches me in a way that hurts me." Helen's aunt went *immediately* to talk to her sister and told Helen's mother she needed to get help right away. Because Helen was able to tell a grownup about being frightened, she helped her whole family.

John was afraid to tell his mother that his father was forcing him to do something that seemed very wrong. He thought what was happening must be his fault and that his mother would call him a liar and punish him. His grades in school got worse and worse, and he began to get sick quite often, with terrible headaches and nightmares. The pediatrician insisted that his mother take him to see a child psychologist where he could talk about his feelings. Finally John felt safe enough to tell his awful secret. Dr. Rosen said, "John, this is *not your fault*. I will have to talk to your parents, and all of you must get help. You need to know that no one has a right to do such things to a child, and your father must understand that he is a sick person."

In John's case, his father denied everything, and finally his mother and father got a divorce. The information did break up John's family, but the psychologist and John's mother knew that some things that happen to a child can be worse than a divorce.

When Parents Change

Another kind of fear occurs when a parent seems to change a great deal over a short period of time. Of course, everyone has good and bad moods. Both children and grownups can be happy and pleasant one day, and miserable and mean the next day. Sometimes mood changes have a physical cause, such as when some women get weepy or short-tempered for a few days each month before having a menstrual period. Sometimes the changes are due to outside influences, such as having a fight with a friend or failing a test or losing a job or having a teacher who you know doesn't like you. Just reading a newspaper or watching the news on television may change a person from happy to sad or frightened.

But some changes are very dramatic and very confusing. David's mother, who usually seemed pretty happy and cheerful, would suddenly begin to cry and would go in her room and do nothing for days or weeks at a time. And then, later, she'd seem fine again. David kept wondering what he was doing to cause these changes. The truth is that David had nothing at all to do with his mother's behavior. She had a mental illness called "manic depression." Usually people who are sometimes *very* sad and then become *very* happy can be helped by a doctor, but David had no way of knowing that. The doctors were trying to find the right medicine to help his mother and were also helping her to understand her feelings. But nobody told David what was going on, so he was very frightened.

Sherryl notices that her father is getting more and more depressed. A year after his steel plant had been closed, he still hasn't found a new job. For the first few months he got up every morning, shaved, got dressed in his suit and shirt and tie, and went off with the "Help Wanted" ads from the newspaper. After three or four months he began to sleep later and just work around the house. Now he doesn't even bother to get dressed but sits around the house in his bathrobe, watching television. Sherryl isn't sure about what's wrong, but she knows her father is acting strangely, and she's frightened.

In a situation like this, it is *normal* to be frightened. Sherryl's father is seriously depressed. The only thing Sherryl can do with her fear is to talk about her feelings to her mother and teachers and other adults. It is *not* normal, however, for any child to feel that he or she can do anything about such a big problem. Only grownups can help with something like this.

Sometimes a parent may start to say funny things that don't seem to make any sense, or will look strange and far away, or will make strange gestures. This may be another mental illness, usually called schizophrenia. Sometimes a person with this illness may need to go to a hospital for a while or even quite a long time. Just remember that a child is *never* responsible for a parent's becoming so ill.

When parents do things that just frighten you for a short time and are soon forgotten, that is a normal part of growing up. But when parents frighten you in ways that are quite terrifying and when this goes on for days and days, it is time to help yourself as well as your family by turning to other grownups for assistance.

When Parents Make You Feel Bad about Yourself

Oliver's mother was very hurt when Oliver forgot to give her a card or a present on Mother's Day. She said, "I guess you just don't care about me. No matter how hard I try to be a good mother, you don't show any concern for my feelings."

When you are a child, you often believe something a parent says, without thinking about it. Oliver felt very sorry that he hadn't thought about Mother's Day as being important to his mother and wondered if he was a mean and selfish person. But the truth is that he hardly ever forgets to put out the garbage twice a week, and he cleans up his room every Saturday morning whether he thinks it needs cleaning up or not, and he brings the groceries in from the car when his mother goes to the supermarket. He's not a thoughtless or irresponsible person at all. His mother was really making a bigger fuss than seemed logical about something that was important to her but not to Oliver.

Instead of accepting his mother's comments without question, and seeing himself as a bad person, Oliver might say, "I'm really sorry I forgot, but I try to do things that please you and show you I love you." Chances are his mother will then remember the caring things he had done.

There are even times when most children wonder if

their parents really wanted to have children. When Ron hears his father talking to his grandmother on the phone and hears him say, "It would have been a much better vacation if we'd sent Ron to camp," he decides it's true, his parents wish he'd never been born. It probably doesn't mean that at all. It's just that parents—all parents—need time to themselves.

Adding to Your Worries

Anyone who says something about you that you feel is true can make you feel worse about yourself. I never met anyone who didn't think he or she had serious faults, anyone who really liked everything about him- or herself. Each of us feels self-conscious and embarrassed and unhappy about something; we think we are too shy or too tall or too quiet or too noisy or not popular enough or have hair that is too curly or too straight.

When a parent is critical, those uncomfortable ideas about ourselves seem to be more true than ever. Maybe you wish you could be less excitable and fidgety, and when your father says, "If you don't stop kicking the table leg, you'll be the death of me," you wonder if your having so much energy *could* kill your father, instead of remembering all the times *you* say things you don't really mean.

You know you make mistakes and sometimes can't stop yourself from doing something you're not supposed to do. When parents act as if you have committed a terrible crime, you think maybe they are right, and you'll always be a terrible person.

When Kevin's father tries to help him with a problem in long division, his father gets very impatient, saying things like, "What's the matter with you, are you stupid?" Then his mother says, "Well, I guess he's just dumb like your side of the family!" Kevin begins to think maybe he really *is* too dumb to learn. What he probably won't know until he's grown up is that some people are naturally good at mathematics, while others have trouble with numbers but can write wonderful stories or love to learn about history or will be terrific at sports. Each person is different and has different talents, but when you are a child, many parents and teachers act as if you should be good at everything. You can't be, and that doesn't make you a dumb person. As a child you surely try to do the best you can, but you will never do everything equally well.

Sylvia, who is twelve years old, heard her mother talking to her grandmother on the phone. Her mother was saying, "Well, let's hope she'll lose that baby fat in the next few years!" Sylvia was already very unhappy and self-conscious about being heavier than most of the girls in her class. Hearing her mother talking about it made her feel sad and hopeless, as if she would be fat and ugly her whole life.

When the parents we love and need so much seem dissatisfied with our minds or our bodies, it adds to whatever we don't like about ourselves. If we feel too short or too tall, if we feel shy or clumsy, anything a parent may say that suggests he or she is worried, too, makes us feel terrible about ourselves. All children worry about such things because they want so much to gain the approval of other children.

Parents Don't Always Mean Exactly What They Say

Some parents have no idea how seriously the things they say can be taken by their children. A mother says, "You're too old to be such a crybaby," when you have to go to the doctor for a shot. The truth is, it is normal to cry when you are scared. Or your father might say, "I don't know why you are acting like such a baby," when you don't want to dive off the diving board. You might think, I guess he's right—I'm a coward. The truth is that each child *gets ready* for any new experience in his or her own time. Some children feel ready to dive when they are five or six; others may not feel ready until nine or ten or older.

When I was about ten years old, a camp counselor told me I couldn't get off a diving board until I could dive off it, no matter how long it took. I stayed on that diving board for about three hours, then finally did a knee dive; she settled for that. It was such a terrible experience that even though I am an excellent swimmer, I could never bring myself to dive again. I wasn't ready and that didn't make me a bad person. Some children can learn to read when they are four years old; some children don't learn to read until they are eight. Once they learn they can usually read equally well. Whether one is a faster or slower learner has nothing to do with being stupid, just different, but it is very hard not to feel stupid when a parent wants you to accomplish something you are not ready to do.

When Joe lost his temper and hit his younger sister, his mother got very upset and said, "Do you want to grow up to be a criminal?" Joe really wondered if that was possible, instead of realizing that he didn't know a single family where brothers and sisters didn't get into fights sometimes.

Parents' attitudes toward schoolwork, grades, and marks on tests can make you feel terrible about yourself. Some parents say things like, "If you don't do better in sixth grade, you'll never be able to get into college." You may get a sinking feeling in the pit of your stomach; could this really be true? Will you never be a good student? Will you never be able to do what you love most—become an architect or a marine biologist or a forest ranger? Is it possible your parents may *never* be proud of you?

Many research studies by educators and psychologists have proven that performance in grade school—and often in high school, too—has very little to do with how much and how well a person can learn in college, once something important happens: the moment when you are allowed to work at the subject that you love the most and for which you have a special talent. One study showed that the people who were the most successful in almost every profession had been C students before they were allowed to concentrate on the subject they really cared about.

Elementary and high school programs are aimed at teaching every student about a great many subjects. Since we aren't all talented in the same subjects, we may not do very well in some of them. Later on, when we can choose to study what interests us most, we can learn almost anything we want to know. If someone says, "You'll never amount to anything," because you are a C student, try to remember that many adults became excellent students only after discovering their special talents.

Wanting to Make Your Parents Proud of You

Children worry a great deal about not measuring up to their parents' expectations. We all want so much to be loved and respected by the people we love the most. When a parent says, "I'm very disappointed in you," we may feel as if the whole world is falling apart; the very thing we are most afraid of is happening.

It's the same thing when a parent says, "I *know* you could do better," and you know you are trying as hard as you can. I remember getting a report card in junior high school that said, "Eda could do 50 percent better in math and science and French." *I* knew I was trying as hard as I could, and that report card made me feel hopeless for a long time. I thought, If those teachers are right, then I must be a very stupid person, and my parents must know it, too. When I got to college and was allowed to study child psychology, though, I started making good grades. I didn't suddenly stop being stupid. I had never really been stupid; what I needed was to study something that was exciting and interesting and for which I had a lot of talent. The same thing can happen to you, if you don't let yourself believe that failing at some things when you are growing up means you will never be able to succeed.

What you need to remember, when you feel that nothing you can do will ever satisfy or please your parents, is that in most cases they think that if they tell you about your faults, they can make you do better. The truth is that children—all people, as a matter of fact—do much better when they are praised for the things they do well. The more you try very hard to believe in yourself and know you are a very special person with wonderful and as yet mysterious talents that will emerge as you grow up, the more you appreciate yourself now, then the more friends you will make when you grow up, the more you will love and be loved, and the more you will enjoy and do well at your future work.

People You See Almost Every Day

The strongest and most important relationship during childhood is with your parents. But there are many other people who can influence your feelings. If you think about it for a minute, you will probably be amazed by the numbers of other people who are part of your life. It is rare for them to have as great an importance in your life as your parents, but the way they behave toward you can have a lasting effect on your life, too.

In School

First and foremost are your teachers. Even though I graduated from high school over forty-five years ago, I remember certain teachers very clearly because of the strong feelings I had about them, and the ways they made me feel about myself. There was a gym teacher who always let the student team captains choose their teammates for soccer and hockey and baseball. We all lined up to be chosen, and I was *always* one of the last to be picked because I was clumsy and terrible at team sports. I have never forgiven that teacher for allowing me to feel so miserable, instead of making up the teams herself. But there was another gym teacher who encouraged me to swim and play tennis, both of which I did extremely well, and she helped me feel good about myself.

Then there was the math teacher who scared me and made me feel so ashamed about never being able to understand geometry and algebra, that I would go and hide in the girls' bathroom during tests. There was also Miss Mortenson who said I wrote wonderful stories, and Mr. Lenrow who told me he thought someday I'd be a writer. They made me feel I was a talented person. Mr. Heller made me feel lovable even though I was a terrible French student!

Teachers can have a very important part to play in how we feel about ourselves. While you are going to school you will have the same kinds of experiences I had. Some teachers will help you feel that you are a special person, lovable and interesting, with special gifts; they will make you feel you have a wonderful and adventurous future; they will encourage your curiosity and give you a love of learning. Some teachers will be severe and critical. Some don't really like children. Others would rather be teachers than anything else in the world; they greet each new class with wonder and rejoice at discovering a whole "family" of exciting individuals. Many teachers feel they learn as much from the children in their classes as the children learn from them. Some teachers are so interested in the subjects they teach that you find yourself all excited, even though you thought you hated that subject. Others use only a standard textbook and workbooks, and even though they teach a subject that interests you very much, you find yourself feeling bored.

What Teachers Bring with Them into the Classroom

Teachers, as well as parents and everyone else you will meet, are individuals with totally different background experiences, personalities, and lives at home as adults.

Richard couldn't understand why Mr. Gomez, his fifth-grade teacher, kept picking on him, making fun of him, saying things that seemed to have nothing to do with the schoolwork. One day, when Richard misspelled a word at the blackboard, Mr. Gomez said, "I bet your mother has a mink coat and your father drives a Mercedes." At another time when Richard was getting ready to go home, Mr. Gomez said, "I guess the cook will make your dinner and the maid will have cleaned your room." Richard was so confused and hurt that he told his parents. They went to see the principal, who said that such remarks were inexcusable and she would certainly have a talk with Mr. Gomez.

A few days later Mr. Gomez called Richard's parents and said he would like to talk to them and to Richard. When they met he apologized and said, "I wasn't even aware of what I was saying, but now I realize there is a part of me that feels bitter and angry at the way I grew up. Mrs. Washington [the principal of Richard's school] talked to me about it. Both of us had a very hard time growing up, and she helped me to understand that somehow, without thinking about it, I was blaming some of the children because I never had a father to take care of me and my mother had to work so hard to take care of five children, and because I had to fight gangs in my neighborhood, and I had to work so hard to go to college. I must get over these feelings and I'm going to get help from a psychologist Mrs. Washington recommended."

Richard's father owned a television station and a newspaper. His mother did have a mink coat, his father drove a red convertible, and they lived in a beautiful home.

Richard began to understand how Mr. Gomez could feel angry and jealous of Richard's comfortable life.

Judy couldn't understand what had happened to Mrs. Greenfeld. For the first half of her sixth-grade class, Mrs. Greenfeld seemed like a cheerful, happy person who was very affectionate toward her students. Then she became very mournful and didn't seem to care what was going on. She seemed to want to get away from school as soon as she could. The whole class felt uneasy and confused; what had they done to bring about such a change? Judy's mother was puzzled, too, so one evening she called Mrs. Greenfeld at home and asked if she was feeling all right. Mrs. Greenfeld burst into tears and said that her mother had had an operation for cancer and was dying.

The thing you need to remember is that children are not responsible for the way teachers act—even when children misbehave in the classroom. Not all teachers are equally talented or experienced. Some can do wonderful things even in a class where there may be several troubled and unhappy children who are unable to accept classroom rules. But another teacher, perhaps young and without much experience, may be so nervous that even with a group of children who usually behave very well, the classroom may become noisy and disorganized.

Teachers Are Human Beings, Too

Your teachers are human beings just like you and your parents; they have good moods and bad times; they are influenced by experiences they had long ago as well as by things in their current daily lives. Like your parents, they may be thoughtful and fair and loving one day and somewhat surly and short-tempered the next. These changes need not "drive you crazy" as long as you know you are not responsible.

You *can* make a difference, however. When you don't expect teachers to be perfect and you don't overreact to different moods, and when you report to the principal or your parents if a teacher does something you know is wrong (such as putting a child in a closet for misbehavior, or hitting a child), and when you make an effort to be friendly and cooperative, you can help your teacher and your whole class.

Teachers need their students to help them do a good job. There are times when you can encourage your friends to be more understanding and helpful. Teachers learn very quickly which children in their class are going to help them. It's a good feeling when you can be such a person.

The Principal

When my daughter started school, I often felt uneasy when I met the principal, even though he was a fine and friendly person. I felt as if I were a little girl again, and maybe he would scold me. Many parents feel that way. The reason is that the principals of our childhood were often people we hardly ever saw unless we were being punished and had been sent to the principal's office. Even though no principal had ever been unkind to me, I held them in great awe because they seemed so powerful.

Sometimes we react to people even before we meet them, because we have certain expectations that may not be true at all. Most principals are people who really want to help students grow and learn, but because each one is "the boss of the school" you may be nervous around him or her, especially if your parents have told you stories of being punished when they were young.

Nowadays children usually see the principal at times when they are not in trouble at all, such as at school fairs and assemblies or on special trips or when the principal is just visiting the classroom. And yet, somehow, even when a principal is really a friend, we sometimes get a scary feeling.

One of the most important things about a principal is whether or not he or she is caring and helpful to the teachers. A school where the teachers know the principal respects them and can guide them is usually a happy school. The second most important thing about a principal, if he or she has to punish a student, is whether he or she makes that child feel like a bad person or whether he or she tries to find out what is troubling the child.

Jay and Jack were sent to the principal's office when they got into a fight outside their lockers in the hall. The principal said, "You two have been troublemakers all year. If there is one more complaint about you from your teacher I am going to call your parents and suspend you for a week. You'd better settle down and get to work or you will both be in *big trouble*." Jay and Jack had the same kind of feeling after seeing the principal as they had had before; they were angry, unhappy boys who felt this was just another proof that nobody cared about them. Jay's mother and father were divorced, and his father lived so far away that Jay hadn't seen him for two years. Jack's father couldn't find a job and was too worried and upset to pay any attention to Jack. Chances are that both boys would go on getting in some kind of trouble until somebody paid attention to their problems.

Mr. Brody was a different kind of principal. A nine-year-old girl had come to school with a knife and tried to hurt a teacher. When Teresa was sent to Mr. Brody's office, they sat down on a couch and he put his arm around her. His office window faced a wide river and they sat together quietly, watching the boats. Mr. Brody said, "You must be very upset and angry to try to hurt Ms. Petrocelli. No one is allowed to hurt anyone else in this school, so we need to find out why you are so angry. Let's sit quietly for a few minutes until you calm down, and then we'll have a talk."

Mr. Brody knew that Teresa's mother had gone to jail for forging some checks; he knew that Teresa's father was also in prison for trying to sell drugs to children. He knew that Teresa lived with her grandmother, who went to work in a factory at seven in the morning and never got home before six o'clock at night. It wasn't hard for him to understand how unhappy and angry Teresa must be.

At first Teresa sat very stiffly, with her mouth shut tight. She stared at the ceiling and refused to say a word. Mr. Brody stopped talking and just sat looking at the boats on the river. They sat like that for almost an hour. After a while Mr. Brody said, "I know how much you are hurting. Sometimes anger gets so bad that you have to let it out somewhere. Is that why you tried to hurt Ms. Petrocelli?"

All of a sudden, Teresa let out a loud scream, and then she cried and cried. When she began to quiet down, Mr. Brody hugged her and told her that the school social worker would be coming to school in two days, and she would see to it that Teresa got some help to make her life happier. Meanwhile, instead of going back to her class, she should come into Mr. Brody's office in the morning and he would give her some crayons and paper and other things to do, and she could just stay with him until the social worker came. Teresa was not made to feel she was a bad person, and there was a good chance she would get the help she needed so badly.

Today more and more principals understand the difference between punishment and understanding. They know that children need rules in order to feel safe, just as they need order in the classroom so that teachers can teach and children can learn. But whether a principal is an understanding person or one who frightens you or who seems too strict and unfriendly is not something you can control; the way a principal behaves is also not your fault.

Other People in Your School

The same is true for all the grownups in your school. I remember the nurse in our grade school; I really loved Miss Colvin. All the children in my school felt they could talk to her about anything, and if we got sick in school, she could always make us feel better until someone could come to take us home. When we came back to school, we could tell by her smile and big hug that she was glad to see us. She made us feel we were each very special.

A friend of mine told me that she would never forget the nurse in her junior high school. That nurse never believed a child who said he or she felt sick until she took the child's temperature; she seemed to think all children were liars. The children in that school dreaded the regular examinations that were held each fall because Miss Johnson would embarrass many of them by talking very loudly and saying things like, "You're too fat," or, "My goodness, you haven't grown any taller since last year," or, "You're too skinny, doesn't your mother feed you?" Whether you have a school nurse who is kind and thoughtful or one who makes you feel unhappy and angry doesn't change the person you are. *You* are a special person even if some grownups don't treat you that way.

The same thing goes for all the people in your school. Sometimes the guidance counselor is a person like Mr. Brody, who understands how you feel; sometimes a guidance counselor has to visit twenty different schools and seems only to be interested in how the students behave and whether or not they get good grades. The gym teacher may be the kind of person who likes you even if you strike out in most of the baseball games, or he or she may be the kind of person who clearly has favorites and these are always the children who are excellent at sports. Even the cooks who serve food in the school cafeteria can influence your feelings about yourself. One of them may shout and tell you to hurry up and scold you if you make too much noise. Another seems to know the names of all the children and acts like a mother who is happy to be feeding her children.

No matter which school you go to, there probably will be about five teachers or other grownups in your school whom you will remember for the rest of your life because they made you feel really good about yourself and about learning. There will be some teachers you won't remember much about, and then there will be a few who didn't seem to understand your feelings and made you feel you would never amount to very much. Your job is to understand that people who make you feel bad about yourself are people who, like your parents, have their own problems. Sometimes you have to overlook what they say or do and just remember that you are a good human being.

People Who Live with You at Home

Many of you have relatives who live with you: a grandparent, probably, or perhaps an aunt or an uncle. Sometimes these people add to your happiness because you know they love you a lot. Your grandfather may be teaching you to play chess or your grandmother may knit you the most gorgeous sweater you ever had. But sometimes there are problems, especially if you have no privacy.

Sometimes a grandparent will act like a parent and tell you what to do. Maybe your grandmother wants to take care of the cooking, and your mother and she get into fights about whose home it is, and you feel uneasy. Or your grandfather gets very upset about your table manners. You feel it's quite enough being disciplined by your parents—you don't want anyone else telling you what you can or cannot do.

While you love your grandfather and feel so sorry because, ever since Grandma died, Grandpa just sits in a chair next to the window and cries, this makes you feel embarrassed about ever bringing a friend home from school. Or it may be that your grandmother is a terrible worrier who wants to know exactly when you are coming home; she doesn't approve of girl-and-boy parties, and she thinks you'll get hurt if you are on a soccer team. Her worries can really drive you crazy.

On the other hand, I know about a second-grade teacher who told the children to bring their "favorite thing" to school next day and tell the class why this thing meant so much to them. She expected the children to bring a stuffed animal or a favorite book. One little boy brought his grandmother!

Even more than your own parents, your grandparents lived in a different world when they were young. Many of their ideas and their feelings may seem very old-fashioned to you. They may get very upset when a child uses swear words; when they were young they might have had their mouths washed out with soap for ever daring to say such things. They may be shocked by the fact that you know how babies are conceived; when they were young they may have been told storks brought babies! You may get very impatient and find it hard not to shout at them, and when you feel most angry at them, you may also feel guilty about getting angry. The truth is that when any people live together and have to adjust to each other, they don't love it every minute, even if they love each other.

Sometimes changing the subject can help a lot. Every time Grandma begins to make a speech about the fact that "in her day" no decent twelve-year-old was allowed to wear lipstick, Madeline tries to change the subject. She might say, "That was a long time ago, Grandma. Tell me about when you were young. What else weren't you allowed to do? What did boys and girls do then, before there was television or places like McDonald's or dishwashers?"

Most older people *love* to tell children about their lives. It makes them feel that even after they die, their lives will go on through the stories they have told their grandchildren about what it was like when they were growing up—and fortunately, most children love to hear these stories. Sean said, "Sometimes my grandfather drives me crazy because he thinks all my friends should spend a lot of time talking to him when they come to the house. But other times it's wonderful—he can help me with my history assignments. When we were studying about Ireland, he told me all about the potato famine that made his grandparents come to America. I got an A on my report because I knew so much about 'the Old Country.' "

EIGHT

People You See Often and Know Quite Well

I t is amazing to realize how much contact you have with grownups in so many different ways and places. Since many of these people frequently feel very strongly that they must change you, push you to grow up, it's not too surprising that they can sometimes drive you crazy. It's equally true that you can like or even love them a lot and be glad they care so much about you. These mixed feelings have to do with what I have been talking about all along—every person is different and sometimes hard to understand.

Doctors and Nurses

I can remember dreading going to my doctor's office because every time I went, I got a long lecture about going on a diet. He made me feel as if I must look like a hippopotamus, but when I look at pictures of myself as a child, I can see I was just a little chubby. On the other hand, a time came when I was really quite sick with rheumatic fever, an illness fewer children get now that there are antibiotics. In that long-ago time, I had to go to bed for about half a year, and the same doctor was wonderful to me. He made me feel sure I was going to get better and he came to visit me and told me jokes, and once he even brought me flowers when I had to stay in bed instead of going to an Easter party at my grandmother's house.

When I was a teen-ager, though, this doctor seemed to feel I needed quite a few internal examinations, and I thought he acted very strangely. When I grew up I realized that in addition to all his good qualities, there was one way in which he was a sick person who was abusing me.

What a complicated man! So many different kinds of feelings I had because of him! After I had become an adult, I learned that he was a man who really loved me and my family, but that he had had a very strange and upsetting childhood and that there was quite a lot of mental illness in his family. It made me very sad to hear, later, that he had had to go to a mental hospital because he had become so strange in his behavior. However, when I was a child I didn't understand why he was a person who could make me feel so bad—and then so good—and then so upset and confused. Nor did I know then what I hope you know now, and that is to tell your parents when someone does anything to you that is very upsetting.

Doctors and nurses have a lot to do with how we feel about ourselves. When my daughter was a little girl, we had a wonderful pediatrician named Dr. McKee. Wendy was never afraid to go to her office, and she was very comforting whenever Wendy was sick. One day Wendy cut her hand very badly and we took her to the emergency room of a hospital because she needed stitches. The next week we went to Dr. McKee's office for the stitches to be removed. The nurse said, "Now, Wendy, you don't have to cry—you're a big girl now." At that moment, Dr. McKee came in and said, "Wendy, it's all right to cry. Crying is for when we are scared or hurt or sad." The nurse had made Wendy feel all alone with her fears, and as if she was a coward if she cried. Dr. McKee made her feel her fear was normal and that crying was natural.

Ginger said, "I had to go to a special doctor about whether or not I would need an operation on my back. The doctor had a tape recorder and he talked into the microphone, using all kinds of strange words I didn't understand. He never looked at my face, just at my spine. I felt as if I was a car in a garage having a new carburetor put in by a mechanic, not like a human being with feelings."

If you have ever had to go to a hospital, you already know how different people can cause you to have different feelings. Karen had to have her appendix removed, and a few days later she told her mother that one of the day nurses had brought her a tiny stuffed animal and said, "I know you must feel very uncomfortable and homesick." But a night nurse had been quite nasty when she rang her bell twice, once for a drink of water and once to go to the bathroom. The important question is, Was Karen a different person in the daytime and in the nighttime? Not at all. She was being treated differently, but that had to do with the two nurses and their different attitudes.

Baby-sitters

If you live with a single parent or if both parents work full-time, you may be spending quite a lot of time with baby-sitters. They, too, are completely different individuals, and you may have a wonderful time with one baby-sitter and feel awful with another. If you have a bad time with a baby-sitter, it is very important to tell your parents. We usually had wonderful baby-sitters for our daughter because I chose them very carefully. Her favorite was a woman who had six grown children and who told me, "I want you to know that it's your job to discipline your child. I'm just going to have fun with her!" Wendy knew that when Mrs. Smith came to our house she would be allowed to stay up later and not eat any part of her meal she didn't like. That was fine with me and her father; it was a special time to have fun—like spending a weekend with grandparents—and some rules could be broken.

But when our daughter was a grown woman, she told me that I had made a great big mistake with one baby-sitter, who told her all kinds of weird stories that scared her to death and had a bottle of whiskey in a paper bag that she drank from when they went to the park. Wendy says she was afraid that if she told us we would get angry or not believe her; lots of children feel that way. Of course, it wasn't true and we would have fired that lady right away. Wendy should have told us, and you should tell your parents at once if a baby-sitter does something you feel is wrong.

Some baby-sitters take their jobs very seriously and follow parents' instructions carefully. Some play games with the children they are taking care of. Some baby-sitters invite their friends over to your home and make a lot of noise. Some baby-sitters yell a lot, and some let you do things about which you know your parents would be very upset. It is important to understand that baby-sitters can also influence how you feel about yourself and that you don't have to—you *shouldn't*—keep it a secret if you feel unhappy or angry or scared with any baby-sitter.

Special Teachers

Most children now seem to have some activities after school or on weekends that they enjoy a lot and others that they feel they have to do because their parents want them to. Alexander had begged his parents to let him take piano lessons from the time he was five years old. When they finally agreed, just about his happiest hours during the week were practicing and taking lessons from a teacher who said he was "a natural."

On the other hand, when Larry was a little boy his mother insisted that he take violin lessons. He was about the most unmusical child who ever lived. He dreaded every minute of the lessons and hated to practice, but the lessons went on for a year. Finally, his mother stayed in the room while he was having a lesson and listened to him play. Afterward she said, "I'm smart enough to know when something is hopeless. No more lessons!"

Sometimes parents have ambitions and dreams they were never able to fulfill, and so they want to give their children the opportunities they missed. The town in which Gordon's father grew up didn't have a Little League team and he'd always felt very bad about that. Now he wanted his daughter to have the opportunity he'd missed. Unfortunately she was far more interested in music and reading. She hated the competition and the disappointment everyone felt when she was responsible for low scores. Finally she began to cry and beg her father to let her drop out. She told her father, "I can't make up for what you missed. Why don't you go be a coach for the team?" Although her father was disappointed, he realized she'd given him a good idea.

I go to swim at a YMCA pool and I try to avoid the times when there are children's classes because I get very upset. Many of the parents and teachers want the children to show off, be the best, win the races, pass the tests. I can see there are lots of children who love both swimming and the competition. I also see some miserable children who are not enjoying themselves at all but want desperately to make their teachers and parents happy. I wish that both the teachers and the parents would try to find out what activities these children would really enjoy for *themselves*. I feel sure there are children in that pool who wish they could join a science club or would love to go hiking or would like to try some painting. As I watch, I think to myself, I hope those children will get a chance to do the things they enjoy and won't insist on their own children having experiences they feel they missed!

There is one special problem about camp counselors or any sort of athletic instructors. They may seem quite grown up to you, but actually to older adults they some-times seem very young and inexperienced. And as I watch some young camp counselors, I notice that they may be more likely to say mean things to the children or punish too severely. I think there are logical explanations for this. Because they may be young and inexperienced, they may feel insecure and have to prove they are in charge. In addition, because they are so close in age to the children in their groups, they may treat them like younger brothers or sisters; at camp they may have more power than they have at home. Also, the younger young adults are, the less they can remember of their own childhood. It's just too close, and for quite a few years they forget anything unpleasant that happened to them as children.

If we are lucky we are able to remember more and more as we grow older. By the time parents and others are more mature, they usually will remember what hurt their feelings or made them think they were bad. At the very time when you are most sensitive to what other people think of you, though, you may have counselors or other instructors who are just a few years older than you are and do not remember how they felt when they were your age. If a young counselor upsets you by making fun of you or calling you names or yelling at you about something unimportant, it's a good idea to remind yourself that maybe this person isn't old enough to understand your feelings.

Relatives Who Are Far Away

Next to parents, other close relatives are the most important people in your life. When I was a child, all my close relatives lived near enough so that I could see them very often; the farthest we might have to travel might be an hour on a train. I felt as if there was a warm and loving circle of people around me. Today, on the other hand, it is quite likely that most of your relatives live all over the country. It's more than likely that some uncles and aunts and cousins are people you may only have met once or twice in your life. If you happen to live in Chicago, you may have one set of grandparents living in Florida and the other set living in Oregon.

Few children grow up today feeling they are part of a close family clan. As travel became quicker and easier, companies began to move their employees often. Young adults felt freer to move away from the place in which they grew up in search of a better climate or better jobs. And sometimes grownups decided to move far away from their relatives because they felt that parents and others would interfere too much in their lives. By the time you were born it is more than likely that your family had spread all over the country.

What I see happening today is that families who are not related at all are filling the gap with new neighbors and friends. Often these can be very close relationships. When families move from one part of the country to another, they meet families who are also far away from relatives, and before you know it, you may be calling the woman who lives on the floor below you in your apartment building "Aunt Betty." The new baby-sitter, Mrs. Ortega, is the same age as your grandmother who lives a thousand miles away, and Mrs. Ortega loves you so much, it's almost as good as having your own grandmother close by. Mrs. Ortega may want to hug and kiss you too much (most grandmothers are like that!), but you don't really mind at all when she says, "I always prayed to God to have children, but my husband and I never had any—and now my prayers have been answered because I have a grand-child!"

If you live far away from your relatives, you may see them only once or twice a year on special occasions like a wedding or for Thanksgiving. You may get a good feeling that they love you even without knowing you very well, or you may feel as if they are strangers. Since you spend little time together, each occasion becomes a kind of party, in which everyone is very polite and on their best behavior.

It's hard to feel they are important to your life. There are no serious problems, but there may not be strong feelings of closeness, either.

Relatives Who Live Nearby

If your aunts and uncles and cousins do live nearby, and you see them quite often, that has advantages and disadvantages, too. The closer people are to each other, the more there is a possibility of problems! Jacob said, "I have an uncle who is five years older than my father. He used to boss my father around, and now he does the same thing with me, and it drives me crazy." Sara said, "My mother has a younger sister who was always jealous of my mother. She felt my grandparents loved my mother more than they loved her. Now my family has more money than my aunt's family, and every time we see my aunt she makes sarcastic comments about how expensive my dress must have been, or she talks about how lucky I am to have parents who can afford to send me to camp. It's very uncomfortable. Her children act just the way their mother does—they act as if we can't be friends."

What frequently happens is that your parents and their brothers and sisters still react to each other as they did when they were children, and it influences how they react to you. An aunt may tell you that you are beautiful; she's someone you love and she loves you. You can tell her anything and you know she will keep your secrets. Chances are she and your mother had a loving relationship as they were growing up. Your aunts and uncles on your father's side of the family may make you feel like a wonderful person—they think you are handsome and brilliant. Those eight brothers and sisters grew up with strong family feelings, and because you belong to them, they love you—you don't have to do anything to gain their approval.

It works both ways; relatives can be your best friends or they can make you feel uneasy. They can provide you with wonderful fun like fishing trips or visits to museums, or they may bother you or ignore you. What you need to remember is that *you* are *you*, no matter how they behave.

Grandparents

Chances are that you have a very special kind of feeling for your grandparents and that they love you so much that you don't feel you have to earn their love. They love you just because you were born and are part of their family. You are their future; you are a very special gift. Grandparents say this all the time. They say, "It's much more fun to be a grandparent than it ever was to be a parent. We don't have to worry about making our grandchildren do well in school or be good. That's their parents' business. We just have fun together." Usually you feel the same way about your grandparents. It's likely that more than anyone else in your life, they make you feel like a wonderful, lovable person.

But it isn't always that way. Ruth's father is Jewish and her mother grew up Catholic. Both sets of parents were violently opposed to the marriage. Her father's family came to the wedding but were very unhappy. Her mother's parents didn't speak to the young couple until Ruth was born. Becoming grandparents was too happy an event, and everyone made up, but the trouble is that each set of grandparents is constantly trying to influence Ruth to believe what they believe. Ruth's father's family wants her to learn about Jewish history and to celebrate Jewish holidays. Her mother's parents give her many expensive presents for Christmas and take her to church whenever she visits them. Ruth feels uncomfortable as each set of grandparents seems to be pulling her in different directions.

Ruth needs to understand that they all love her and feel they are doing what is right. It will be kind and caring if she tries to learn about and enjoy what each wants her to know. Actually, that will enrich her understanding and her life, and will help her to make her own decisions when she is older. Instead of feeling torn in half, there would be much less strain if she let all her grandparents know she respects their ideas and feelings and wants to learn from all of them.

It is wonderful to know a grandparent loves you, but sometimes grandparents love too much—you feel stifled and exasperated. Grandfather may feel hurt if you'd rather be with your friends than spend more of your time with him. He doesn't seem to understand how important it is for you to be with people your own age. Or Grandmother may be very disappointed if you don't get all A's, having conveniently forgotten that neither she nor her daughter ever could accomplish that. You are so special that she wants you to be perfect, so she offers you bribes to get good marks. You know that would make your parents very angry and it makes you angry, too.

If a grandparent says or does anything that you feel is really wrong, you need to tell your parents. If what grandparents do or say is different from what your parents think but not too important, it is probably wise just to listen politely and not make a fuss. You need to remember that grandparents are individuals, too. Each of them grew up in a different way in a different family and has some qualities that you like and some that may upset you.

It is important to remember that when people get older, it becomes harder to change their ideas. They also get tired more quickly. It doesn't mean Grandma loves you less when she can't play as many card games with you as she used to.

It's upsetting to see grandparents change as you grow up. It is very frightening if they get sick, and of course it feels terrible if one of them dies. Whenever you feel worried or sad, let your parents know and tell them you need to share your feelings with them. If a grandparent becomes very sick or dies, you need time to feel your grief and sorrow, and you can expect to feel very upset for a long time.

Sometimes you may get the feeling that your grandparents can't possibly love you because they move far away, perhaps to a warmer climate. Sometimes they are working so hard you don't see them very often even if they live nearby. Or they may travel a lot or start to play golf or spend a lot of time walking or doing exercises. None of these things is a sign that they don't love their grandchildren. They are signs that life changes, and at each stage of life people have to adapt and do what they feel they need to do in order to live long and healthy lives.

There is a story about a porcupine family who lived at the foot of a tree. When it was cold they wanted to get close to each other to keep warm, but if they got too close to each other, their quills would get in the way and hurt them. That's how it is with people. We need each other for love, but sometimes, if we get too close and don't give each other enough room, we get scratched. It's often that way with all of us, grandparents included.

People You See Often but Don't Know Very Well

It's strange to think that you see the crossing guard on every school day, but unless he or she is a neighbor or a friend of your family, you probably don't know anything about this person. The same thing is probably true of the school bus driver or people who live on your street or the salesmen in the store where your parents buy your shoes or the people at the checkout counter at the supermarket where your mother and father go shopping.

Hurt Feelings

If these people whom you see often but don't really know are pleasant and friendly and you don't do or say anything that bothers them, chances are they won't "drive you crazy." But sometimes things *do* happen that make these people important to you.

Justin and two of his seventh-grade schoolmates decided to have a race down the street, and in their excitement, they didn't quite stop at the curb where the school guard was posted. She began yelling at them. She said, "What's the matter with you ruffians? Maybe your parents wouldn't mind if you all got killed!" All of a sudden, just having some fun sounded like a crime. If the guard had said, "You *must* stop at the curb or you might get hurt," Justin and his friends probably would have agreed that they should be more careful, but instead they felt angry and frightened. When you don't know anything about a person, he or she can upset you quite easily.

What Justin and his friends couldn't have known about that particular school guard was that her seventeen-year-old son was a cocaine addict and had run away from home when his parents tried to get him to go for medical help. Her heart was broken, and she also felt both anger and guilt about being the parent of a seriously troubled young man. Justin and his friends happened to be the target of all her bad feelings that morning. Actually, except for being thoughtless sometimes, they were great kids. When we don't know why someone is very critical and says mean things, we need to remember we don't know what problems they may be having, and they don't know anything about us, either.

Angela is a very shy person, and even though she's eight years old, she still sucks her thumb when she feels nervous or embarrassed. When she was shopping with her mother at the supermarket, the checkout lady said, "Boy, do *you* have a lot of freckles!" She didn't mean to be cruel, but Angela hates her freckles. Feeling upset, she put her thumb in her mouth. Then the checkout lady said, "My goodness, you're too big to be sucking your thumb." Turning to Angela's mother, she said, "Is this your little baby girl?" If Angela had been alone, she would have felt terrible. Luckily her mother answered, "We love Angela's freckles and she's not a baby. You just made her feel shy." The checkout lady looked angry and didn't say another word. People who make fun of a child are probably people who had the same thing done to them when they were children. We need to remember it's their problem, not ours.

Different Attitudes

Howard and his friends had been sitting at their desks in school for so many hours that by the time they got to the school bus, they were very restless and jumpy. They got silly on the bus and started giggling and jumping from one seat to the other. The bus driver, who had three school-age sons, very quietly pulled the bus off the road and said, "I can't drive safely when you kids get wild and noisy. We'll just sit here until you can calm down. As soon as you get home you can play." The children calmed down very quickly. They felt the bus driver was their friend and that what he was asking was reasonable.

The year before, that very same group had been made to feel that they were impossible children. That year the bus driver was an older woman who happened to be very nervous. She didn't have any children of her own and the children on the bus seemed unmanageable to her. If anyone made any noise, or changed his or her seat, Miss Farley would start to cry. The children felt frightened and were convinced that they really were what she called them: "rotten, mean brats."

The way a person treats us can give us different views of ourselves, and we have to remember that the difference is usually in the other person, not in ourselves.

Attitudes about many things can be influenced by neighbors, too. The woman who lived next door to Julie was the mother of a little boy who had been run over by a truck and killed. Every time Mrs. Pollacheck saw Julie she would warn her about crossing the street and say, "You could get killed and break your mother's heart." Julie began to wonder if she should ask one of her parents to walk her to school. She would get a funny feeling in her stomach whenever her mother sent her on an errand where she had to cross several busy intersections. She even thought, Doesn't my mother care if I get killed?

On her birthday her father said he thought she was now old enough to ride her bike to school and Julie burst into tears. She told her parents what Mrs. Pollacheck kept telling her all the time. They told her that Mrs. Pollacheck felt guilty about her son, and her grief was all she could think about. By trying to be very protective of other children, she felt a little less guilty for not watching her own child, even though the accident was entirely the fault of the truck driver who hadn't stopped at a red light. Her parents helped Julie realize that growing up includes taking a certain amount of risks; if we don't take risks, we'll never be able to do anything.

Special Problems

There are some people about whom you need to tell your parents or some other adult immediately.

Harry often saw a man walking around the playground in the park near his house. The man was always alone and never spoke to anyone. Harry paid no attention to him until one day Harry was leaving the park and the man stood in front of him and opened his raincoat. The man didn't have any clothes on underneath his coat. That is a person who is sick in his feelings and needs help. Harry needed to tell his parents immediately so they could call the police, even though Harry might have felt sorry for the man and not wanted anyone to hurt him. At one time people who exposed themselves in public might have been sent to jail. But now the police and the courts know this is an illness and will try to get this man to a mental hospital where he may be able to get well.

Rachel noticed that an older boy, whom she'd seen in her neighborhood many times, sometimes stood right out in front of her school at three o'clock. She figured that maybe he was waiting for a younger brother or sister. One day, when she started out the door, she saw this boy hand a white envelope to one of her classmates, who gave the boy some money. Just that week in her classroom she had seen a film about drug pushers who try to get schoolchildren to buy drugs. She ran home as fast as she could and told her parents, who called the police. There are some strangers who are dangerous, and you need to get grownups to help.

Florence saw the man who rented a room in her friend Freda's house driving around the school quite often when school was over for the day. She thought that he might be calling for Freda. He seemed like a nice, friendly person when she met him while visiting Freda's house. One day, when Florence was halfway home on a street where no one else was walking, Mr. Williams pulled his car up and offered to take Florence for an ice cream soda and then drive her home. Her parents had told her *never* to get into anyone's car. Florence hesitated for a minute—after all, this was somebody she knew—but decided to say, "No, thank you." She just had a strange feeling she should walk up to the nearest house and ring the bell. Mr. Williams drove away very quickly. When a woman came to the door, Florence asked if she could call her mother, who came and picked her up. Her mother said, "What you did was absolutely right. Even when it's someone you know, you need to be careful. Mr. Williams really may be just a friendly person, but it's best never to take a chance that it might be some person who is mentally disturbed."

The next day Florence told Freda about Mr. Williams's behavior. Freda looked very funny, almost as if she was going to cry. She said, "Can I come to your house after school? I need to tell you a secret." That afternoon Freda told Florence that Mr. Williams made her very uncomfortable. He was always trying to pat her legs under the dining room table and he would try to make her sit on his lap when no one else was at home and he would hug her and kiss her in a way she didn't think was right. Florence said, "You have to tell your mother," but Freda said she couldn't. Freda's father had left home and Freda's mother needed the money Mr. Williams paid for his room.

Florence felt that Freda had a very serious problem, so even though she felt like a tattletale she told her parents all about what Freda had told her. Her mother said, "Darling, you were right to tell us. Freda is in danger and we must help her. Just let us take care of it." Her parents went to visit Freda's mother, who was very, very upset to hear what had been happening. A few days later Freda's mother told her, "Mr. Williams has to move to another city for a new job, so we are going to sell this house and find a small apartment." Freda was very relieved, but she was worried about Mr. Williams. When she asked if he was all right, her mother said, "He's going to see a doctor who can help him find out why he makes you and your friend Florence uncomfortable."

Whether someone who behaves in upsetting ways is a stranger or a parent or a grandparent or an aunt or an uncle or anyone else, a child is not being a tattletale when he or she feels the need for special help from other grownups because something or someone seems strange and dangerous.

People You May Never Meet and Never Know

This chapter is different in one way from any of the other chapters in this book. It is about grownups who may very well "drive you crazy," but you may never see them or even know that they are influencing you.

Martin is twelve years old, and one day, looking in the mirror, he is horrified to notice that there are several pimples on his chin. He immediately feels ugly and is sure his friends will be disgusted by his appearance. He probably reacts this way for two reasons—the first is that any young person approaching adolescence feels insecure about his or her appearance, but the second and equally important reason is that people who manufacture salves and creams for acne want to sell their products.

When I was a child there was no television. The only advertisements were on radio and in magazines and newspapers. There was a man who was called "Uncle Don" on a children's program, and once I sent away to the program for some Japanese stationery that was a great disappointment. But I don't remember any advertisements that really influenced the way I thought. Television, however, brought about the creation of hundreds of very powerful advertising agencies, and all of them are trying to make people like Martin want what they have to sell.

Advertising agencies often employ psychologists to tell them about how children feel. They know that you want to be popular; they know you are not yet strong enough to like the idea of being different from anyone else. They know that if they advertise whatever they are selling in a very attractive way, and make it seem that no child should ever be without it, children will try hard to make their parents buy a certain brand of blue jeans or a particular cereal or some toy based on one of the Saturday-morning cartoons.

Grownups are influenced by television advertising, too, but they are less likely to buy something unless they feel it will be useful, and if it turns out to be something they don't like, they won't buy it again. Grownups also want to feel that they are keeping up with the fashions, however, and even they may not realize how many of their choices are made for them, in very subtle ways. There is nothing wrong with wanting things that you like, but it is a good idea to understand that what you like may be decided for you by very clever advertising.

Martin's fears are very useful to the people who want to sell him something. He wants to be attractive and popular. When he sees and hears something on television about how terrible it is to have pimples, his worries are greatly increased. Even though his family doctor may talk to him about the normal hormonal changes that are going on in his body, and tell him that almost every kid in his class is going to have the same problems, Martin doesn't listen. The advertising has upset him so much that he can't hear anything else.

What I hope you will begin to think about is whether

some of the people who influence your feelings don't really care about you at all.

What We Need to Know about Advertisements

Imagine that you are in a big office building at a meeting of people who want to sell a new toy: a space rocket that "can destroy a whole city with one death ray." At the meeting, a woman says, "Both boys and girls want to feel powerful. They want their friends to think that they are winners. Children feel insecure as they face all the changes that will come in the next few years. This rocket will give them a sense of power, and they will definitely want it for Christmas." A man says, "We need to have a very strong campaign, showing this rocket during every commercial break on the Saturday and Sunday TV cartoons." The president of the toy company says, "I want a full report on the cost of making this rocket and how we should set the price. Let's figure out how long we can keep it on the market and what we can expect in the way of profits."

Nobody is talking about what message this advertising campaign will give to children. Is this a toy that will encourage children to use their imagination? Does it make war and killing seem like a good thing? Will children want to play with it for a week? A month? An hour? Is the price going to be a great hardship for some of the families whose children will beg and beg for it?

These are not questions that advertisers ask; they are interested only in *making money*. And they can make you want what they are selling so much that you feel as if you'll go crazy if you don't have it.

It's important to think about *why* people on television

or radio or in magazines want you to buy something and to understand that they are only interested in you because you might become a customer. The truth is that many of the things advertisers say to children are not true. One kind of vitamins won't make you healthier than any other kind; a plastic toy may come apart easily; a particular cereal may taste good but have so much sugar in it that it is not good for you.

Action for Children's Television

There is an organization of parents and teachers and others who do care, very much, about children. Its name is "Action for Children's Television," and it was started many years ago to protect young people from misleading and upsetting advertisements as well as to promote good television programs. This group is responsible for such things as seeing to it that no one advertises a toy on television that needs batteries without saying so. And no advertiser can say that just eating some cereal is an adequate breakfast; now they must at least show pictures of such other essential foods as milk and orange juice. Members of this group meet with television producers and members of Congress to try to get better programs and laws that will make advertising more honest. For further information, you can write to Action for Children's Television, 46 Austen Street, Newtonville, Massachusetts 02160.

Famous People in Advertising

Sometimes an advertisement will include the appearance of someone you know and admire, such as a baseball player or a movie star. Some famous people are very careful; they will not recommend any item unless they are sure it is safe and worthwhile. But other "stars" are more interested in making a great deal of money and will recommend anything for which they are paid. If you find that someone you admire is promoting a product that turns out to be very unsatisfactory, it might be a good idea to write a letter, letting this person know how you feel.

The important thing is to realize that it is up to you to decide when people are being honest and fair and when they may be using you in some way. This is a difficult task. It is much easier to judge people you know in situations where you can see what they are doing. But you can make better choices if you come to understand some of the problems.

Watching Television

For example, it may seem very exciting when in a television show you see cars racing and leaping through crowded city streets and over bridges and crashing into each other, or if you watch a program on which ten or fifteen people are shot and killed. You may forget this is all make-believe. In these cases the message you are getting is that human beings don't matter and that life is not sacred. It is important to think about whether or not the producers of these programs (whom you don't know) are interested in helping you to become good citizens.

Adventure, even a certain amount of violence, may be entertaining and exciting, but it's a good idea to balance the kinds of programs you choose to watch. There are also some excellent television programs that can give you a sense of awe and wonder about the universe, or help you understand science and medicine and space travel. There are lovely programs about wild animals and birds, about ecology and astronomy and foreign countries, all of which encourage you to become more curious about the world around you. There are important programs that help you understand yourself and other people, some of them carefully and thoughtfully designed to help you to deal with such problems as divorce or the death of a friend or living with an alcoholic parent or cheating at school.

You need to be aware of the fact that television producers are almost always more concerned with "ratings" than anything else. In New York City, for example, newspapers and television programs make so much of the very few terrible things going on, that residents and visitors probably think it is a very dangerous place all the time. The truth is that despite overcrowding, noise, not enough homes for everyone, poverty, and unemployment, close to 11 million people *don't* hurt each other and do struggle to be decent. Only a small minority are involved in acts of violence, and even within that small number, most of the violence occurs among people who know each other, within the family or the immediate neighborhood.

If you turn on a local news program, and the first report is about a murder in Australia or a bank robbery in Canada, you can be sure that the news department was desperate to find something *terrible* on which to report. On that particular day, there must have been no muggings and no murders in your area.

The broadcasters want to catch our attention, and they know that it is violence that accomplishes this most quickly. If they were to start a program by telling about people who were helping to feed hungry children or about how a fire was avoided because someone did *not*

112

smoke in bed, no one would pay attention. The reason we always hear about bad things happening is that these are rare enough to be news.

Of course, you need not become suspicious of everyone or of everything you see or hear. What will be most helpful is trying to become well informed so that you can make better and better choices. There are many wonderful people you never see who really care about you: educators, mental health specialists, people in government concerned with child welfare, religious leaders, and many others. These are people who are doing everything they can to make life better for children and their families. But there are others who are thinking about themselves and not anyone else.

As you grow up, one of your most important jobs is to find out which groups of people you want to believe and can trust. It's not an easy job, but the more you try to understand all the kinds of influences there are in your life, the less strangers will be able to drive you crazy by confusing and upsetting you.

The Grownup *You* Would Like to Be

I asked some children what kind of parents they wanted to be when they grew up. I imagine you can guess some of the things they said! They were never going to yell at their children, and they would not make them go to bed early, and they would never take away their children's privileges to watch television. They would never make their children eat anything they didn't like, and they wouldn't nag their children to do their homework.

Can you guess what I said? Chances are they will do a lot of those things! But when you become a parent you will realize that there are some unpleasant things you have to do to help children learn how to be safe and to get along with others. You also will do some of the very things you don't like your parents to do because sometimes you won't be able to help yourself—your parents will have had such a strong influence on you that you will be a lot like them. In addition, I never met a single person who didn't get tired, cranky, and impatient some of the time. Nobody ever grows up to be a perfect person.

Repeating Childhood Experiences

When I was a little girl, my mother used to make a terrible fuss about my cleaning up my room on Saturday mornings. Sometimes she'd get so angry at the mess that she'd just push all my toys and books and games off the shelf and tell me to put everything away all over again. I remember standing in the middle of the room after she went out and muttering under my breath, "I'll *never* treat a child this way!" Guess what? When my daughter's room got to be a terrible mess, I would storm into the room and behave just like my mother. But I really didn't want to be that kind of mother, so I spent a lot of time talking about my childhood to a psychologist until I could stop repeating things I was doing only because of the way my parents had acted.

Fortunately for my daughter, her father didn't grow up with parents who were too fussy about messy rooms, and so he would say, "Come on, Wendy, let's go to the playground—your mother is a little crazy this morning."

He was very fussy about table manners, though, because his parents had made him behave at mealtimes. Sometimes he would shout, "*Civilize up!*" so loudly it made Wendy and me jump. Then I would try to make him understand he was being unreasonable.

When you grow up you, too, will find it hard not to do the same things your parents did that drove you crazy. Some of those things won't matter too much. Maybe you get very annoyed when a parent discusses you with another person as if you weren't in the room, so in the future you will try to be more sensitive about a child's feelings—but maybe you will forget how you felt. However, there are some things your parents might be doing—things that are frightening and wrong—which it is *very important* for you not to do when you grow up.

One of the things we have learned is that children of alcoholic parents frequently become alcoholics themselves. We also know that parents who abuse their children were almost always abused children themselves. Edward says he wants to break that cycle. He asked his gym teacher (his favorite teacher) if he could help him find a group Eddie had heard about for children whose parents have serious problems. His teacher said, "Eddie, I'm so glad you asked me. I know you once mentioned you think your parents drink too much. If you want me to, I'll introduce you to an Al-Anon group for kids your age." Whatever serious problem parents may be having, such as becoming violent, or taking dangerous drugs, or crying all the time, there are now groups all over the country to help their children.

I also asked some children what kind of teachers and doctors and baby-sitters and police officers they would like to be. Can you guess what they said? They wanted all grownups to be polite and friendly and understanding! It's a *big* order! A good one, but never entirely possible. By now, I hope you have realized that parents as well as other grownups have complicated personalities and problems and can't ever be perfect.

Learning to Love Yourself

Until recently, children felt that whenever parents or other adults mistreated children, it was because children were bad. If the children got beaten, it was because they deserved it; if they got yelled at, it was because they were wrong. Too many children grew up—and perhaps you now know them as grownups—feeling that every punishment was deserved. Children grew up not liking themselves. No matter how hard they might try to please their parents and teachers—or their husbands and wives and bosses when they grew up—there was always that feeling, "I'm not really a good person."

People who feel that way—who are not able to love themselves—have a very hard time loving anyone else. You have to have felt that you were loved in order to express love to others. So the very first thing I hope you will learn while you are growing up is that you are a special and lovable person. That doesn't mean you are perfect! It means that you are a human being, and from the moment you were born you had all kinds of wonderful things you might someday do, already inside you.

Sometimes you may do something wrong; you may not be able to stop yourself from saying something mean or taking something that doesn't belong to you; you may drive your parents crazy by making too much noise or not getting up on time in the morning or leaving your bicycle in the driveway. But these are all normal things that are part of growing up, and they don't make you a bad person—just a young person.

When People Try Hard to Be Better

For over forty years I have been meeting and talking with parents and other people who live and work with children: thousands of parents and teachers and principals and nurses and doctors and counselors. Looking back, I cannot think of a single person who didn't *want* to do a better job in helping children to become happy, useful grownups.

This doesn't mean they were always able to succeed. An extreme example would be the many parents I have met who had spent time in prison for different crimes. They were meeting with me because they desperately wanted to be better parents than theirs had been. They knew that lack of love and guidance and too much anger and abuse had made them grow up hating themselves, and they begged me to help them be better parents to their children. I sometimes cried when I heard their stories.

One man, who had been left on the doorstep of a church when he was two months old and lived in a series of very poor foster homes where he was often beaten, ended up in an Industrial Home when he was twelve years old. That's a place for "junior criminals," too young to be sent to regular prisons. Artie was sent there because the foster mother he was then living with was beating a two-year-old girl. He had gotten a kitchen knife and threatened to use it if she didn't stop hurting the baby. No one believed him. At the Industrial Home, Artie learned all kinds of criminal skills from other inmates. After many years in prisons for different crimes, he was involved in an armed robbery where a man was killed, and Artie was sentenced to twenty-seven years in prison.

In this prison he met a priest who was also a psychologist, and began talking to him about his life. Father James gave him the affection he had been craving all his life and helped him to understand and to care about himself. Artie realized that he had always hated himself and everyone else, and hadn't really cared what happened to him. He had always felt worthless: a terrible person whom nobody would ever love.

When he finally came out of prison, he married and he and his wife had a baby. They joined a group of ex-convicts who were talking with me about raising children. The first thing Artie said to me was, "Eda, please, please help me to be the kind of father I needed and never had. I want my baby to know how lovable she is, and that no matter what she might do, we would never stop loving her!" Here was someone who had had a terrible life and yet wanted so much to be a good parent.

Some parents and teachers and others seem to understand children and know what they need, most of the time. Others want to do the best for their children, but things that happened to them when they were children have made them upset, confused, unable to express loving feelings. But I cannot remember ever meeting any grownup who *wanted* to hurt a child. They all wanted me to help them understand children and become better human beings themselves.

No one grows up to be a perfect person. To a greater or lesser degree, all the grownups you know experienced some things that hurt them when they were children. It is unlikely that there will ever be a time when children or adults can be patient and understanding and kind all the time. People get tired and disappointed and confused and angry and sad because life is often difficult. Human beings can try to do the best they can, but they can never succeed completely. It's the *trying* that is so important, so brave.

To Be a Good Human Being

The most important thing you can learn as you are growing up is that you are an important and lovable person, special and different from everyone else. You are surely not going to succeed at everything you try to do or everything grownups want you to do, but, no matter what, you are lovable.

In order to feel that way, you need to try to understand that the grownups in your life need to feel lovable, too, and maybe they often don't feel that way. When parents have bad feelings about themselves, they may try hard to make their children perfect—and that is when they drive you crazy. They want you to make up for all the things they don't like in themselves.

You will probably make your children go to bed too early and eat things they don't like and punish them by taking away their television time. Those are not the most important things. What I hope most of all is that you will know you are a good human being who tries very hard to become a better human being all the time, and that you will let your children know that no matter what childish things they may do, you will always love them and want to help them.

Many years ago, I met with a group of policemen. (It was long before we began to realize that women could work in this field as well as men.) These were policemen who were assigned to work with "juveniles." Officer Rogers said, "Several years ago, I was called to come to a certain address where a gang of school kids were throwing rocks at the windows of a half-built, unoccupied house. When I got there, they were running away, but I caught up with them, and frankly, I gave them hell! I screamed they were no-good, rotten, worthless kids and would probably end up in jail. I threatened to book them if they got into any more trouble. They slunk away without a word."

Officer Rogers was now taking special college courses in which he was learning about children. He added, "If something like that happened now, I would let the kids know they were breaking the law, but then I'd sit down with them and find out what was bothering them, and I'd try to get to know each kid. If I could be their friend, chances are they might become less angry and not want to destroy other people's property."

Someone asked our daughter, when she was grown up, what it had been like living with parents who were both psychologists. She said, "They made a lot of mistakes just like any other parents, but I always knew they were trying very hard to be better, wiser people." We felt proud of that. In most cases your parents and teachers and other grownups you know also are making mistakes but are trying the best they can.

I hope you will try to understand the grownups around you better, and that this will help you to try to be the best person you can possibly be. People who are trying hard to understand themselves and others are the best parents. And whether or not you become a parent, self-understanding and self-esteem will surely lead to your becoming a terrific grownup person.